The Colour of God

Andrew Thurlow

The story, all names, characters, and incidents portrayed in this production are fictitious. No identification with actual persons (living, or deceased, or reincarnated), places, buildings, and products is intended or should be inferred.

That being said, the Dalai Lama is, of course, real and irreplaceable.

King Charles was, up until recently, Prince Charles; whether the two are the same person or not remains to be seen, but there is a chance that a full remodel was done behind the scenes and that somewhere inside the King, is in fact a comedic Prince Charles, dying to get out.

The head of Scientology in the UK is coincidentally named David and had a wife named Shelley but that's not this David or the spectre of this Shelley.

It's worth a mention that Douglas Adams has corporeally left us, but thankfully he blessed us with writings that will be forever relevant and intelligently humorous.

Dave Chappelle is mentioned as the global benchmark for being "The Closer" but doesn't appear in the book.

Ben Elton is also mentioned as someone potentially better at telling a story than Dave Chappelle, but that is opinion and not necessarily fact.

The front and back cover art is created by Andrew Thurlow using the AI at NightCafe https://creator.nightcafe.studio As per the terms and conditions of the Nightcafe platform, the rights to the images are the ownership of Andrew Thurlow as "the creator". See https://creator.nightcafe.studio/faqfor more information. The flags montage is also created by Andrew Thurlow using more traditional image manipulation techniques. The copyright for each flag, obviously, remains with the respective institution.

For my lovely wife Trang

For your patience, listening, and valiant attempts to understand and sympathise.

Contents

Chapter One

The Bishop

Jessica's life was of her own construction.

As life wasn't particularly busy, she had yearned for days that were a little bit spiced up.

Clearly she had not been listening when told to be careful what she wished for.

Days floated by with an air of monotony, which, in her experience, was to be expected in the church. Jessica had certainly been warned when looking at theology as a vocation. Along the way, one of her fellow students equated it to war. A lot of boring stuff like moving, digging, building, and preparing, followed by moments of sheer terror before returning to a repeat of the mundane.

If you managed to survive.

She hadn't always wanted to be religious. It wasn't so much a calling, as a falling into it.

While studying at Oxford, Jessica had taken a Theology and Philosophy class with one of her friends. She was studying the arts with the thought of leading into psychology, but during that class she found Theology particularly interesting. Her family had pious leanings, but never to the point of encouraging their only daughter to go into the business of religion.

The look on her Mother's face was priceless.

She had moved her course away from the arts and majored in Religion and Theology. After graduation, she took on some local religious activities at the big Anglican Hospital and pushed her studies back a bit. The local Bishop was so nice to her, encouraging her to go back and complete her studies and become ordained.

Now, as the Bishop, as she sat on the park bench outside the church, waiting for the parish priest to bring some tea, she understood why. Even the heartland of the Anglican faith was suffering from what can only be considered apathy. Empty pews in churches, empty beds in hospitals, and empty seats in schools. Even the poor weren't interested in church handouts anymore, thanks to those well-meaning non-denominational charities propped up by the government. Priests, like the nice Reverend Michael she was meeting with now, weren't leaving in droves, but the erosion of the ranks was very evident. The rejuvenation the church had enjoyed for centuries just wasn't there anymore.

So here she was, about to have a nice conversation with a 65-year-old, trying to encourage him to stay on for another decade so they could keep the lights on at this ornate 600-year-old church.

Michael came out holding two steaming cups of tea. It was a glorious day in the south-east of England, with bright blue skies and a crisp breeze listlessly meandering off the Cambrian Mountains.

"Sorry for the hold-up," Michael said apologetically. "I had some solar panels put in at the rectory," he snorted slightly to provide the poorly hidden sign he was about to tell a funny story.

"You would think on beautiful sunny days like today they would be working their magic at a great rate. But the power was out, so I had to double back and stoke up the wood fire in the range in the Vicar's room."

Michael guffawed shallowly, looking her in the eye and lowering his voice as if a secret needed to be told.

"Hardly encouraging when we are using fossil fuels to compensate for technology failures," He laughed boisterously.

"God will provide." Jessica joined his laughter.

"Oh Yes. Nobody said God had to provide solar." Michael's laughter clamoured across the small garden in a valiant effort to remind the parish that the church still had spirit.

Jessica paused and brought her own laughter back to a light smile.

"Seriously Michael. It's wood, not a fossil fuel, and you shouldn't be putting in solar panels anyway."

"Really?" Michael replied. "What's the problem? The deal was awfully good; it was government-sponsored, like they were giving away free electricity. When it works."

He smiled again, recalling his previously witty remark.

"Yes, I see." Jessica pursed her lips slightly to make her best school ma'am face.

"However, it doesn't send a good message to the parishioners about faith, does it?"

Michael looked at her quizzically and asked, "How do you mean?"

"Well," she continued, "The Greens are the ones stealing our flock. Selling the faithful the line that the fate of the planet is in their hands and they can change the outcome by changing how they act and what they do. Change outcomes that are in God's hands, through technology. Then, when things go wrong, the greens blame climate change and say we need to do more to stop these natural disasters. They bang on about doing things differently, which is invariably the green way."

Michael nodded noncommittally.

"Whatever happened to faith in God, Michael?" She aimed the last question squarely at him, like he was a contestant on Mastermind.

"Well, yes." he bumbled. "I'd never quite looked at it that way."

Jessica blew a breath over the teacup and watched the steam flatten away from her before taking a small sip, just enough to test the heat and the quality.

"Beautiful cup of tea, Michael," she complimented him. "Made through God's provision to boot."

"Yes," he replied, almost reaching a Kaa-the-Python hiss.

"So, be a good chap and have them removed."

Jessica had her very matter-of-fact tone ramped up.

"You can send the bill to my office, and we will settle it so your parish books don't get out of whack. If you can make a song and dance about it for the parishioners, you know, 'They don't work; we should trust in God's plan'. That would be great."

Michael's face could have been plastered on, like one of those busking still-life actors in the mall on weekends. He very clearly had more questions but was experienced enough to know this was not the time to ask them.

"To help out long-term, I will redirect some of the building preservation grant money to your parish, which should allow you to lead this beautiful old building forward." Jessica smiled willfully. "It needs a kindly, guiding hand to show the devoted in the community we are still here to help them with questions of faith."

"Great." Michael didn't know what the building preservation grant was. He had been custodian of this parish and this church for thirty five years, and no one had told him he had money to spend on building works.

"Now. That's not what I came for." Jessica took another long sip of tea.

The cup had become room temperature, and she had about two minutes until that extremely fresh breeze made it unpalatable.

"Yes." Michael exhaled; he knew that was the sideshow. Jessica always came with the sideshow first.

"You know our troubles filling parish positions. It's no secret."

Jessica took a breath and made a face like she had just lost a loved one.

"Parish numbers are down in all forty-two Dioceses. Flock and shepherd," she elaborated.

It wasn't the first of these conversations she'd had to have.

"We simply can't find the presiding hands we need from the flock, and we need our long-serving shepherds to hold the line with us at the breach while we suffer through these troubling times."

Jessica was a little over dramatic, but Michael was from an era where that sort of thing seemed to work.

"Yes, absolutely," he said, looking like he was about to lift from his seat and shout hurrah.

"So we were hoping we could find a way for you to stay on past your 65th birthday and manage the church and the parish for another ten years or so, while we train a replacement."

That was the crux of it.

Jessica was a little unsure who the 'we' were. She supposed she could say her and God.

Maybe a little presumptuous.

"Well..." Michael seemed like he had something to add but was too nervous to spit it out. "Carol and I had some plans to take a trip." He seemed to fumble with his words, stopping to drink some tea to bolster his resolve.

"A sort of pilgrimage."

"Great," Jessica could see her in. From here, she was the expert, playing off money, faith, and duty.

"I can arrange a stand-in for a while, say three months, while you and Carol take that pilgrimage."

Jessica felt Michael's tenuous resolve waver.

"If it's somewhere religious, we can even help out with some funds."

"Really." Michael seemed a little lost for words.

After years of being told there are no funds, now they seem to have risen from some magic pots hidden in the garden in Canterbury for three different things.

"Wonderful. Yes," Jessica loaded him up some more. "For a guardian of the faith who needs some time to recharge his batteries, it's the least that we could do."

"I'll have to talk to Carol, but that sounds great" Michael replied nervously.

Done. To beat the bicycle rush around Oxford, she needed to get on the road.

"Great! You talk with Carol. Oh, sorry, Michael, that's my mobile." The scheduled alarm Jessica had set before the meeting went off in her bag with refined precision.

"No problems," Michael coughed, "You know your way out. I'll take care of these cups." His voice wafted off as she made for the car, feigning an important call from another Bishop.

"I'll just get the mobile on Bluetooth," she shouted as she closed the car door and started the engine.

The ageing Audi S6 shrieked into action. The car noise was enough to drown out anything else, but Jessica feigned the call until she was out of sight and then made for the motorway.

Right, she thought to herself, another Houdini move. If she could get Michael over the line, she would have seven hundred parish priests for the eight hundred and ten active churches in the Oxford Diocese. Many of those churches were not full-service; some couldn't even muster a Sunday sermon, but all provided weddings, funerals, christenings, and baptisms on demand.

The money spinners, she smiled.

She felt a little like a rare wildlife cataloger photographing a dying breed mating.

Jessica allowed the warm glow to wash over her, confident that she had saved another piece of British history from demise. How many other parishes and faiths had sold off old churches as restaurants, function centres, and even oversized family homes, not to make ends meet but because they simply couldn't keep bodies on those key services?

The church would always find money from old benefactors and the newly deceased. Those who like to leave their money in some faint hope of a last-minute redemption. But ordained people on the ground were a rarity that hen's teeth would be happy to be compared against.

'What was the answer?' she pondered. 'I suppose that should be a question for God.'

Jessica wasn't sure, but having been in the business for over twenty years, she figured God kind of left it to them.

The hierarchy.

Maybe something to take up with the Archbishop next time they have lunch.

The hands-free in her car rang. The display on the dashboard showed it was the Bishop's office calling, so she answered.

"Jessica speaking," she enunciated deeply to ensure the detail made it over the Audi's engine and road noise.

"Yes, hello, Bishop. This is Rosie from the office." Rosemary was her new office assistant.

"Yes, Rosemary. How are you dear?" Jessica needed to be nice; it was hard to find anyone in the office who would work for the wage she paid. She wanted them to have faith, but that seemed to be a luxury in this economy.

"Great. Thanks, everything is under control here." Rosemary was sounding positive, but clearly, there was something not quite right.

"Good to hear. What can I do for you?" Jessica enquired.

"Well, I had a call from the Vicar in Reading just now." Rosemary was trying to get something out but wasn't sure how to dislodge it from her throat. "A call of a somewhat difficult nature."

"No problems. I can call Peter directly if that helps." Jessica just couldn't be bothered extracting whatever it was out of Rosemary for Peter to have to re-explain it later, and from the car, she was wired, or is that wireless? Maybe the right word was connected.

Jessica wasn't sure.

"Great," Rosemary said, sounding like she had just escaped the noose. "I'll go back to my knitting then, figuratively speaking."

"Thanks. I should be back in the office within the hour, the Lord willing and the traffic allowing."

Jessica didn't wait for a reply and hung up.

What would Peter have that was so urgent? She scrolled through her address book using the steering wheel controls and found Peter Reading on the list. Peter was a bumbler and a bit of a panic merchant.

He had probably burned his toast.

The phone rang five times before he picked it up.

"Oxford Diocese. This is Peter."

"Very professional, Peter," Jessica said, complimenting him on his phone-answering manner.

"Yes. Well. Thank you, Bishop." Peter shuffled through the words like he was talking under the surface of a glue pot.

"What seems to be the problem? You spooked Rosemary in my office, but I thought I would get the details directly from you." Jessica needed to minimise Peter's speaking parts to speed things up. The A40 was a reasonable trip around Oxford, but she didn't want Peter taking up all of it."

"Yes. Well. So, as you may recall, we had submitted plans to place a new modern church in Newtown. That suburb that has recently been developed near Reading," Peter glaciated the answer.

"I do," Jessica said, to the point. "We recognised a gap where there was no religious representation in that area from any faith."

"Yes. Well," Peter continued, "The submission went to a quarterly council planning committee that asked for more information in the form of a public consultation to report back at the next meeting. We offered to run it, but they said they wanted to run it themselves."

"Indeed," Jessica replied, "I would have preferred we had some control, but it is what it is."

"Yes. Well." Peter was finally coming to the point. "Turns out yesterday was the date of the meeting, and the consultation was tabled. Our submission was rejected. Rejected because the people consulted overwhelmingly agreed that having a church in the neighbourhood would bring the wrong sort of people into the area."

Jessica almost bit her tongue. "They what!"

Peter's confirmation came out like a canal barge moving through the fog. "Yes."

"It's one of those new neighbourhoods," he said, pushing on and wading through a molasses of words. "The suburb is full of people who are transitioning, of mixed race, or part of those blended families. Most of them earning money through the new economy. Not our demographic, it seems."

"A whole suburb says WE are the wrong type of people!" Jessica exclaimed, "Hard-working, generous, God-fearing Christians!"

She took a breath, knowing full well that Peter wouldn't be quick enough to interrupt.

"How can we possibly be the wrong type of people?" It was a rhetorical question that Peter didn't need to answer.

"Be a dear and send me through the paperwork. I will get together with the team and put together a reply. What sort of time do we have?" she quizzed Peter.

"Well, yes," he coughed slightly at the thought of the time pressure, "the next meeting is in three months, and they have said if they receive nothing they will consider the matter closed."

"Thank you, Peter." Jessica replied, "You've done a great job so far, but leave it to the head office now; we will take it from here. Have a great day. Don't fret about this; I'll handle it." She quickly hung up before Peter could add anything more.

She shook her head.

Not the right type of people.

How can a house of prayer for good English Anglicans not be welcome on the outskirts of London? It is the heartland of England. She resolved to read the planning committee's documentation on the matter thoroughly. She would bring in legal counsel to check that there isn't some new kind of religious persecution going on.

She pulled off the A40 at Cutteslowe and made her way up Banbury/Oxford Road until the familiar sights of the care home and Langford Lane came into view. She did love Oxfordshire, and was not giving up on Berkshire either. Why did she feel she was in a fight for the livelihood she had chosen? Maybe this is how typesetters, toshers, or phrenologists felt in the days before their vocations disappeared with a puff of smoke into a new economy.

God was God, and that wouldn't change, but if churches didn't exist, then how would they encourage people to use Anglican schools, Anglican hospitals, and Anglican aged care homes? People might even start praying in their own homes; what a wasted opportunity that would present. The Anglican Church was so deeply ingrained in England's history that if it ceased to be now, how would the tapestry of England's history continue?

Jessica parked in her designated car park and made her way up the steps to the usual stream of greetings from the staff at Church House.

She replied to each one magnanimously.

"Yes, Good Afternoon."

"Yes, Lovely Day."

"Yes, they are beautiful flowers at the entrance."

Every member of her staff was very spiritual, and they were lovely people, but naggingly, she felt this was a dogfight, and they had brought the miniature poodle set to the ring. She made a further mental note to take this up with the Archbishop. Jessica finally made her way into her office.

She had an open door policy, so she left the door open.

Standing at the desk she wiggled her mouse to get her computer screen to come to life. She sat down with her mobile phone up to her face to get the device to unlock and then found her two-factor authentication app. She punched the code and her password into the computer, and she was in.

After the successful cyberattack eight months ago, the diocese tightened things up significantly. Jessica was not so much guilty, as complicit in the final decision to not tighten security after the 2018 security report, which made it clear they were vulnerable. The final choice was taken by the Archbishop on financial grounds, but she had agreed it was unlikely they would be a cyberattack target. Needless to say, they hadn't even noticed that they had been compromised until the ransom demand came. If not for the brilliant work of the IT support company they had hired, which added immutable cloud backups, they would have been in real trouble. They rewarded that company by giving them a contract to perform a full security upgrade and extending the long-term support agreement, but the result was a long login process that was taking most of the staff quite a while to get used to.

Her email was overflowing.

Jessica was particularly interested in anything to do with the interfaith conference she had been organising. Her inbox was mostly cluttered with office banter, but she did see a few responses from the Catholics giving early confirmation and one from the Dalai Lama's private secretary confirming his attendance and his willingness to be a speaker.

Wonderful.

Jessica quickly replied to the private secretary, thanking him and advising that the speaking part would be on day two, early in the morning. The theme was interfaith and unity; she would be happy to write out some notes for his Holiness, or if he would like to just speak on the subject, that is more than fine too. There would be delegates from every faith present, so her suggestion was to keep it fairly open.

The truth was, Jessica knew the Dalai Lama would speak beautifully. She had seen him speak a few times. He was inspiring. She had the King to open on day one and the Dalai Lama on day two, so all she needed was someone galvanising for day three, preferably to open the day rather than close the conference.

Day three was intended to be a short day so people could make travel plans. They often wandered off at different times anyway.

One of the other emails was from the venue in London. A checklist of things they provide for the three-day event, including furniture, IT equipment, lighting, menus of the meals being presented, availability of the rooms for setup, and security. It was a 35-page document. There was a lot to consider, as faiths all came with different dietary and prayer requirements, and they all needed to make those prayers at certain times.

The last thing Jessica wanted was a whole contingent getting up and heading out because the speaker had run over prayer time or, worse, meal time.

She scanned through the list. The east-facing prayer hall, Halal food, and no music in the lobby for Muslims. No pork for the Jews. Vegan for the Buddhists and Hindus. All ladies at the function centre must wear a head scarf unless they were part of another faith delegation that was offended by wearing a head scarf. All ladies, including those of other delegations, must dress appropriately with covered arms, torso, and legs. There is no smoking throughout the lobby, auditorium, eating halls, or private meeting rooms, but there is a smoking area that incorporates a small indoor room and a large outdoor area with seating if the weather is fine.

"Great," Jessica said in a positive voice out loud, "we'll call it an interfaith smoking area."

"Is everything OK, Bishop?" Rosemary inquired from the door.

"Yes, thank you, Rosemary. Everything is perfect." Jessica replied, "I got the details from the venue, and it's ideal. All fits in with what I saw when I visited last year, and all within budget."

"That's fantastic," Rosemary replied enthusiastically. The Bishop was going to like Rosemary; she had a very positive personality.

The whole Interfaith Conference budget came from a grant Jessica submitted to the UK government during the COVID-19 lockdown. She needed to keep herself busy, so she started looking at data on the decline of organised religion to cheer herself up. Jessica noticed that it inversely matched the data on the growth in green policy. She checked and found there was a huge explosion in the number of green members of parliament around the world, driving government policies pandering to the 'Climate Change Emergency.' On the back of that comparison, she cooked up this scheme to take back the initiative for the faiths.

Jessica had thought carefully about how to get all the different religions to agree on a path forward.

At first, she thought it would depend on what that path forward was. Later, she decided it didn't matter what the path was; they would never all agree.

In her mind, it became a numbers game.

If the Catholics and Orthodox would join with Anglicans and other protestants, they would hold 33% of the faithful. If that could actually happen, then she just needed one other major faith to be in it to get over 50%. The Buddhists only held 7%; if she could now get the Dalai Lama to back the plan, then maybe they would all join in, and hopefully the Hindus could then be persuaded. Hindus make up 16% of the world's faithful. There is no way the Hindus from India were going to move fast enough, but if she could lock in some local Hindus, they might be able to push them along. The Muslims, with 24% of the faithful, were very organised when they weren't infighting. But she had to be honest with herself; the Muslims were not so likely to join, even if it was a great plan. The Muslims just wouldn't join anything Christian unless someone charismatic from the ranks could unite them and show them this was their chance to take Allah to the world. There was a London imam she had similar discussions with at the last interfaith conference who seemed like he had some sway.

No doubt there were lots of balls in the air that could land any way.

May we live in exciting times, Jessica thought.

Jessica opened another email this time from the Mahant at BAPS Shri Swaminarayan Mandir.

BAPS is the shortening of the *Bochasanwasi Shri Akshar Purushottam Swaminarayan Sanstha*, which is a Hindu denomination within the *Swaminarayan Sampradaya. Swaminarayan Sampradaya*, also known as *Swaminarayan Hinduism* or the *Swaminarayan* movement, is a Hindu *Vaishnava Sampradaya* rooted in *Ramanuja's Vishishtadvaita* and characterised by the worship of its charismatic founder *Sahajanand* Swami, better known as *Swaminarayan*.

So you can see why they like the acronym BAPS.

The *mandir* or temple is also known as the Neasden Temple, as it is in the London suburb of Neasden. Neasden is old Anglo-Saxon for 'the nose-shaped hill', which seems a little less spiritual, although the nose-shaped hill temple does roll off the tongue quite nicely.

The Mahant was sending an email to see if Jessica was interested in the work of a PhD student from Cambridge, a very bright girl who was studying Future Infrastructure and Built environments with a focus on sustainable living. The Mahant outlined that this may particularly interest the Bishop as her plan includes the ability to stop worrying so much about climate change. As a girl of faith, her thesis calls on the religions of the world to unite and focus on changing government policy in the right way, not the usual green-washed rubbish.

"I'm all ears," Jessica thought. Then she considered that she may also be all eyes and fingers, as it was an email.

The interfaith conference at the moment had no backbone and was in danger of just becoming another bloated talk fest. Her best chance of eeking out an actual plan was Marcus the Marketing Guru, but if she was honest with herself, he was more of a doer once the decisions were made, a motivator, a can-do guy who could mobilise. The actual plan had yet to be decided on, so maybe some brains are what is needed.

"Cambridge, eh?" Jessica said it out loud.

"Rosemary," she called out. Rosemary appeared quickly at the door.

"Yes Bishop," Rosemary replied in a chirpy voice.

"I am forwarding you the contact details of a young lady called Maryam at Cambridge. I would very much appreciate it if you could contact her and arrange a meeting between the two of us. I have some time tomorrow, if she can spare me an hour. I will drive, so you will need to book me out most of the day as it's a two-hour drive each way. You can move the eleven a.m. meeting with Helen to the following day, and you can cancel the phone meeting with Peter, as I have spoken to him this morning. That should leave me with an open calendar. If she's not free, please try to find a time when she is and arrange it. I need it done ASAP. OK."

"Yes, Bishop," Rosemary said, turning and heading back to her desk.

"Make it in that nice cycling coffee shop. I'll need a good coffee after the drive."

"Right-o," Rosemary replied.

Jessica was impressed. Usually, after that much information, there would be twenty questions from her previous office assistants.

If she can pull things like this off, Rosemary might just be worth her weight in gold.

Chapter Two

The Imam

Sunan al-Tirmidhi, Hadith: 2612

Hasan hadn't let the gravity of the situation consume him.

London's largest Muslim community centre had been shut down again by the Metropolitan Police over safety concerns.

He was a little surprised that the whole thing needed to be closed.

Yes, there had been some very minor problems with some of the men, who had used the mosque to pray, being newly returned from the IS Caliphate in Iraq. But how was he to know that? Two thousand worshippers came in daily to seek absolution and consolation from Allah, not to spread hate.

It was very hard to impress that on the police, especially the task force police that had shut everything down. They saw all the followers of Islam as the problem, not just a few.

Hasan was hoping he could make some sense of why everything had been shut down. He would also like to know why the police were so sure it was part of an endemic problem, as the superintendent had so wilfully sprayed all over the morning news.

Hasan pulled around in front of the Wood Green Police Station in his C63 Mercedes. He loved time in his C63; the twin-turbo four-litre V8 was music beyond compare. He circled the controlled parking zone, looking for the possibility that a resident had taken their car out for the day. Unlikely, it must be said, as most residents now took the tube or bus and left the car at home. Parking was a nightmare wherever you went in London. The recently added Ultra Low Emission Zones didn't help. They made transiting, unless you owned a bicycle or an electric vehicle, almost impossible. He wasn't ready to give up just yet, as he lived and worked in the same borough, so he felt like this was part of his turf.

Hasan must have spent a good ten pounds in petrol driving around looking for a car park. He was just about ready to head for the Just Park website to reserve something that would cost him at least another twenty, when, Allah be praised, a sweet young lady came out of her house, jumped in her Prius, and drove away, leaving an open bay for him. It was just a small walk to the station, so this spot would be perfect.

His control of the brutal power of the Mercedes was delicate, and he navigated into the tight space left by the Prius with finesse. He was a master of the reverse park. No assist, no camera, just good old-fashioned spatial awareness and know-how. He sat for a moment to thank the Almighty and listen to the end of the news report from BBC 1. The story on the community centre closure was second behind a BBC investigation into the maltreatment of show dogs.

Was there nothing else newsworthy in this country?

He took the few steps up to the doors of Wood Green Police Station with vigour and reached for the handle. A constable coming out eyeballed him very rigorously, taking a very aggressive stance and waiting for Hasan to open the door and enter before making his way out.

Did he not have any respect for his elders? Hasan must have been twice his age. Did he also not recognise Hasan's robes as those of an imam?

Indignation has so many faces in this world.

Hasan let it wash over him, as he had come for business. He had decided to make this trip alone, whereas normally he would come with an entourage. He wanted to achieve a peaceful understanding with the police rather than create a standoff.

The auxiliary on the desk looked up from her computer with the start of a smile on her face, which quickly turned into a very hard-bitten, almost anodyne expression.

What did he do? Hasan pondered. He opened his arms in a gesture of peace and watched with horror as her face showed just a modicum of fear.

"Young lady. I am the Imam of the North London Community Centre and part of the London Council of Imams." Hasan handed her his card, which she turned over hoping to find an English version. Her face returned to the bloodless gaze she had formerly held, allowing the fear to retreat for the moment.

"Yes Sir. How can I help you today?"

Ah. 'Sir'. Hasan repeated the words in his mind. Maybe he was finally getting some respect.

"I am here to discuss the matter of the closing of the Community centre and associated facilities this morning. The Superintendent left this card with one of the muezzins."

"Yes. Sir. Please take a seat in the waiting room. The Superintendent is in a meeting currently but is scheduled to be out shortly, and I am sure he will want to talk to you."

"Very well." Hasan wasn't happy with waiting, but he did understand his scheduled arrival time could not be known.

He turned to the waiting room and noticed the huge no-smoking sign on the door. To leave no doubt and circumvent any language barrier, the no-smoking picture was reiterated in bold letters in Arabic. He laughed internally as the message was then repeated in smaller letters underneath in French. Clearly, the French addition was a necessity, tacked on as an afterthought.

"Excuse me, young lady." Hasan smiled warmly. He needed to smoke.

"I see the sign saying no smoking in this room. Is there a place I can smoke close by?"

"All smoking is banned in government buildings," she replied curtly. "The High Street is designated smoke-free, but you could go into the park across the road. Make sure you use the assigned smoking area, which you'll find closer to Newham Road, past the playground."

"Thank you, young lady. Can I also ask the estimated time the Superintendent may come out of his meeting? So I can make sure I am back here should he come looking for me."

Her face looked a little perturbed to be asked, but she turned back to her computer monitor and, without making eye contact with Hasan, read out the time.

"Meeting is scheduled to be complete at eleven a.m., in twenty-five minutes."

The phone on the desk rang, and without reference to Hasan, she picked it up.

Hasan shook his head at the rudeness. How simple is it to offer an 'excuse me' he thought.

"Yes Billy. Everything is OK. There is no need. Thank you."

Hasan didn't wait to be insulted again and turned to exit the building. Twenty-five minutes should be plenty of time for a quick cigarette.

He exited the station and crossed the High Road to walk down Earlham Grove to the parkside entrance. The park appeared to be primarily there for the George Meehan House. He walked past the first two benches and was greeted by huge signs stipulating what you and your dog were NOT allowed to do at this spot. He pushed on past the playground, as the auxiliary had noted, and found a bench furthest away from the station that had no signs on it or around it.

Allah be praised; this must be the one, he thought to himself.

He took out his silver-plated cigarette case, which was a gift from his wife, and extracted a cigarette, which he lit and inhaled. The noise was quite bad, as the bench was located next to a basketball court at the primary school, and it looked like the whole school was less playing basketball and more screeching at each other.

He drew heavily on the cigarette, drawing as much nicotine into his lungs as he could and holding his breath to fully savour the moment.

"Excuse me," he heard faintly from behind him.

The imam had been given the choice between facing the child's playground of the George Meehan house, the houses on Earlham Grove, or the school. He was a thoughtful man, so he had chosen to position himself towards the houses in case anyone thought he was inappropriately looking at children.

"Excuse Me." There again, but much louder and more aggressively framed.

He turned to see a slightly built, very pasty man standing up against the fence of the basketball court.

"That smoke is travelling over to the basketball court." The man's voice was at the whine level of broken power steering in a TVR Chimaera.

"You really shouldn't smoke near children. Very thoughtless."

Hasan was not one to shout, so he took a few steps towards the man, who promptly moved back from the fence two steps and then held his ground.

"I apologise, young man. While I am from North London. I am not familiar with this area in particular. I was told by the Police Auxiliary at Wood Green Police Station." He pointed over his shoulder and continued, "that this is an appropriate place to have a cigarette. I mean no harm to anyone, and I would be happy to find an alternative place if you are more familiar with the area and can point one out to me."

"What!?!" The man wasn't able to hear anything Hasan had said.

Hasan took a few more steps forward but stopped when he saw the man's expression.

"I don't want any trouble," the pasty man shouted again. "You just shouldn't be smoking near children."

Hasan was not a stupid man. He quickly extinguished his cigarette, raised his hands in a sign of peace, and nodded gently.

"My most humble apologies."

He turned to walk away and looked at his watch, a gold Rolex, a gift from his father. With fifteen minutes until the Superintendent would be finished with his meeting, Hasan estimated the time it would take him to get back to his car from Earlham Grove and decided that might be the better option. He walked with a little extra pace and prepared his cigarette as he approached the car, lighting it and entering the car all in one fluid movement.

Hasan put on the radio to see if there was a news update, scanning the channels, hopefully looking for a bulletin. Nothing but music. There was pop music; rock music; pop-rock music; electronic dance music; dance-pop music; indie rock; country pop; pop rap; and even hip-hop. He found BBC News Radio, which had crossed over to a puff piece on the growing importance of hip-hop and rap to inner-city Muslim teenagers.

What!

Hasan listened carefully, drawing wilfully on his cigarette to channel his disgust at the disrespect shown by the reporter to the faithful. He made a note to lodge a complaint with the BBC.

Having finished his cigarette, now just a limp butt he had sucked the life out of, he opened the door and discarded the remains in the drain.

He looked up at his watch to check the time. His hand was level with but not in the focal range of the sign stating that the drain goes to the Thames River.

Eight minutes, just enough to get back even if the Superintendent comes straight from his meeting to see him.

He didn't rush but made good time back to Wood Green Police Station and spent less than a minute in the waiting room before the Superintendent came in.

"Imam Hasan. Thank you for coming in. I'm Superintendent Terrance Allan."

At last, someone knew at least a little bit about how to address him respectfully.

"Ah. Superintendent, thank you for seeing me so promptly. I hope we can resolve this matter that so regretfully occurred this morning."

"Right. Well. First, let's move to an interview room, shall we?"

"Yes. Of course." Hasan had dealings with the police before, but usually as part of an entourage, placing some good words in for youth that had deviated from the path to embrace the decadence of this modern world.

He followed the superintendent past the auxiliary desk and into an area that had a group of interview rooms. The young lady auxiliary on the main desk had been replaced by a very large young male, who provided him with a look that could only be called disdain as he passed.

"Room 17b." The young auxiliary called out to the superintendent.

The Superintendent nodded and opened the door with his swipe card. Waiting inside was another officer, who, for the moment, didn't identify himself.

Hasan sat, feeling like perhaps he should have arranged that entourage after all.

The other man kept his head down and made no effort to engage.

How very rude.

"Now." The Superintendent placed his neatly bound paperwork on the table and began, "Is Mohammed Aalim Habib known to you?" Without waiting, the Superintendent continued. "or Junaid Naeem Aalam or Zahid Akbar Sahil."

Hasan was a little unsure of the question.

"Respectfully, Superintendent, I am not aware of these individuals. I surmise that they are three of the two thousand worshippers that passed through our doors yesterday. I am unsure if they are frequent worshippers or if this is their first visit to our holy mosque."

The Superintendent raised an eyebrow suspiciously. Hasan continued.

"I am here to formally request that we open the community centre, nursery, mosque, elderly and youth support centres, and medical centre to allow them to serve our community again as soon as possible. Our people need these services daily."

Hasan emphasised the second "our" by opening his arms to encompass the Superintendent and the man seated at the desk as well.

"How can we do that when you are harbouring known terrorists?" The man seated at the table cut in with a very aggressive tone.

"With all due respect, as we have not been formally introduced," Hasan again widened his hands in a show of peace. "The community centre does not harbour known terrorists. We have over twenty instances this year where we have assisted The Met with investigations into men who have lost their way and were seduced by the promises of the IS Caliphate."

Hasan had taken on many of those cases personally. He was a highly educated, peaceful man who had no time for these reckless fools. He enjoyed England and wanted to protect all it had to offer, assist the community, and spread the word.

"Murphy, Islamic Anti-Terrorist Squad."

The man didn't make eye contact, but Hasan was not one to be bullied.

"You must be new in this area. I will help you. As a man in your position, you should make it your business to know that the correct way to address an Imam is Imam, followed by their first name. In my case, I am Imam Hasan. Perhaps your learned colleague can assist you." Hasan nodded at the Superintendent as a sign of gratitude for showing respect during their initial introductions.

"If we are going to work together to stop these wicked individuals from causing chaos on the streets of England and from bringing shame on our peace-loving religion, we must start by respecting each other and addressing each other appropriately, Mr. Murphy."

Hasan was not aggressive; he had a goal he was trying to achieve, and he knew there were many ways to do this. It was clear to Hasan that Mr. Murphy did not share his goal, so he appealed to the Superintendent with a shrug.

"Superintendent Allan. Might I ask what further information you require from me to achieve my goal of reopening the vital services we provide to London's largest Muslim community?" Hasan continued. "I do not know these names. You know that we share the information we keep on our community databases with The Met. I have no doubt you have cross-checked and found them not to be on our lists. They are not people we want to associate with. If we can provide further assistance, we will."

"You need to start collecting ID from all the people attending the mosque." Murphy's tone was unchanged: "We need preregistration with verified photographic identification to be presented at each attendance."

Hasan was a little taken aback.

"With all due respect, Mr. Murphy. That is ridiculous; this is England. No religious group of any denomination is subject to such administrative overheads. Would the Catholics allow this? The Anglicans? The Jews?"

Hasan came here today to fight for his people, but now he felt he wasn't just defending his faith but all the faiths right to gather.

"Right. Well. That's not constructive in the circumstances." Superintendent Allan cut in. "You are correct; we haven't been able to find any evidence that you are aware of the history or movement of these men. But our facial recognition surveillance picked them up entering the mosque, and no corresponding footage was found with them leaving, so we had to be thorough. We of course apologise for the inconvenience to your community, but our first duty is to the people of London."

Hasan was again a little surprised that the Met had installed facial recognition without informing his office. He pondered if there was facial surveillance at Westminster Abbey or St. James Cathedral. He thought not. But he should have guessed. While the Muslims of the UK worked hard, went to school, paid tax, and lived and died shoulder to shoulder with other faiths, the Met regularly singled them out for special treatment.

"Thank you, Superintendent, for your calm head in these troubled times." Hasan focused hard on his goal and let the bigger picture blend into the background of a future setting.

"I will openly pledge my support and the support of the community centre to rout out these people who do not embrace the true nature of Islam. But to help the Muslim people of North London, I need you to allow us to reopen immediately. Please. I implore you."

"Yes. Right," The Superintendent seemed a little unsure if he was making the decision or if he was waiting for a higher power. Murphy stared at the table like he might be able to put a hole in it if he stared long enough. He had his say, which was nullified by the ridiculousness of the requests he had made.

"I will put a call to the Sargent on the ground and get things wound up." Superintendent Allan seemed to finally have realised it was his call.

"Thank You, Superintendent. *Rahmat Allah wa Barakaatuh.*" Hasan gave a blessing to a job well done.

"Hey. It's the King's english only in interview rooms." Murphy said finding energy to further embarrass himself.

Hasan stood and made for the door, waiting for the Superintendent to assist in opening it with his swipe card, ignoring Murphy.

"I noticed the no smoking sign in Arabic and French in the waiting room, Superintendent, so please excuse my use of Arabic in blessing our coming together for the common good."

***

Bishop's Opening to C4

Jessica made the run up the M1 to Cambridge fast. Much faster than Google Maps predicted but not exceeding any gazetted speed limits. Well, not deliberately exceeding them, and if any excess was achieved, not being caught, which in all honesty could be considered the same thing.

Maryam was waiting for her at the Espresso Library coffee shop, which was a bit away from the university but made lovely coffee and had a better vibe than the soulless chains of Costa, Starbucks, and Caffe Nero.

The Espresso Library was mostly a coffee shop but also part art history refuge and, finally, part cycling enthusiast hangout. Well, it was Cambridge. A lovely, eclectic, very local mix. Jessica loved everything about Cambridge that was like Oxford. You might say that is everything, unless you are from one of those places or attended one or the other of the universities. There was certainly a fierce rivalry that people not from either of those places perhaps couldn't quite buy into, but Jessica did.

Maryam had arrived already, although she said to Jessica only just, which Jessica just loved. After the initial introductions, Jessica returned to the counter to order Maryam some tea and herself a lovely, fluffy, chocolatey cappuccino. Maryam had sat towards the back, and when returning to sit down, Jessica took a moment to look at some of the art as she passed by. Beautiful, colourful paintings, a great deal about cycling, and some obviously of the Cambridge buildings and skyline. Maybe done by the owner or the owner's friends. As she walked, her eyes were drawn to a pair of cycling shorts, starched and mounted, very colourful and bursting with vivid fluorescent colours. Just as she had looked too long, the huge bulge in the front came into view, and she rather embarrassingly turned her head.

"It takes you by surprise when you get to it." Maryam laughed as Jessica sat at the table. "Everything else is so G-rated, and then the shorts."

"More G-string than G-rated." Jessica laughed.

The two took some time to introduce themselves properly while waiting for the drinks to arrive. Jessica felt instantly at peace with Maryam, who was as clever as she was built up to be. She also seemed to have such high levels of emotional intelligence, compassion, and a deep understanding of the plight of the religious. She seemed to understand that what history had dealt the faiths was not an easy hand. Too many Jacks of Spades, not enough Queens of Hearts, and more Jokers than you can use, but nowhere to discard them.

Maryam spent almost thirty minutes explaining her PhD thesis in a nutshell, following points she knew by heart. Jessica mostly kept silent, but asked some very poignant questions, which Maryam answered in full with an energy and honesty that Jessica found refreshing. Jessica was almost sure Maryam was her girl but needed some further confirmation, so she questioned her.

"Have you done a lot of public speaking?" Jessica spoke in a quiet voice.

"Quite a lot," Maryam said.

"You know the King is opening the forum and the Dalai Lama is speaking on Day Two. The place I have open, which would potentially be for you, would be following the speech by the Dalai Lama."

Maryam went a little red. "Oh wow!" she exclaimed dreamily.

"Yes, it goes straight to your heart, doesn't it?" Jessica knew that look.

"He is, well, even though I am Hindu and he is Buddhist, he is a personal hero of mine. A man of great insight and tolerance."

"I would be honoured," Maryam admitted unreservedly.

"Do you have any video of you speaking publicly?" Jessica asked with moderate concern that maybe the stage lights might get to Maryam.

"I do," said Maryam. "I will send you a few YouTube links, one taken when I spoke at the young scientists conference three months ago. That had an audience of one thousand people. I also have a video of one before COVID-19, when

I was part of the youth and poverty debate in Cambridge. I think that was an even bigger audience."

Jessica was impressed.

"I hear where you are coming from, bishop, but I assure you I am a very confident speaker. Even in the presence of light as bright as the Dalai Lama."

They both smiled.

"Do you mind sending me your presentation?" Jessica asked politely.

"Of course, no problem." Maryam pulled out her phone and quickly fired off her modified presentation.

"It's a bit dumbed down." she admitted. "The original paper is over six hundred pages, bursting with theories, algorithms, proofs, tables, and references. A bit much for most people, but I think you would have no problems. I have a copy with my supervisor being cleared, so I can send it to you when he's done if you like."

"Sounds Wonderful. I love a good read." Jessica smiled again.

What a remarkable girl, she thought.

Chapter Three

The Rabbi

The Ashkenazi Rabbi

Yitzakh was a powerful man.

He had always been well-built in his youth, but while other young Rabbis were praying and hypothesising, he was doing military service and things that made him buff. Other people noticed, mostly girls, but also some of his friends and so, where there was a tendency to let that fall away when studying his *Semikha*, he put in extra effort and did both. To keep buff, he worked out and did Krav Maga. He loved Krav Maga, and as a big guy, a lot of people didn't like to see him as their next opponent when he entered tournaments.

Somehow, deep in his soul, he found a way to find room for Krav Maga and the *Talmud*.

The powerful side was not always the blessing it may have been assumed to be. Many people in the Rabbinic community couldn't see how Yitzakh could have spirituality and pecs. So he more often than not had to convince them of his true calling. He did this through study and by using the words of his ancestors to best counsel the *minyan*. While he was a powerful man capable of dishing out the strongest of rebukes, Yitzakh abhorred violence against non-consenting opponents. He loved the work of being a Rabbi and was always first to be available for judging, legislation, supervision, and teaching. He had no bounds and lots of time.

His good work brought him to the attention of the Ashkenazi Chief Rabbinate, who bought him in to work in that office and also into his confidence. When that Chief Rabbinate's ten years in office were complete, the next Chief kept Yitzakh around as he knew the place, the people, and the form. The following election ten years later saw Yitzakh take the reigns as the Ashkenazi representative on the Chief Rabbinate of Israel. This year was his year for the Presidency, which alternated with the Sephardi Rabbi annually.

As president, he had a few special tasks, but the key job of the Rabbinate was to respond to the *Diaspora* on *Halakhic* questions. There was some organisation to be done, but after twenty years around the other Chief Rabbinates, he had that under control. So mostly, Yitzakh was free to pursue his other passions.

Yitzakh loved technology, especially Israeli technology.

It changed the world, automating and protecting, transforming the desert into a lush garden, and bringing the sea to Israel's doorstep. He marvelled at what Israeli security experts could do, what Israeli medical researchers cooked up, and how Israeli agronomists achieved plant yields no one else could seem to achieve. He immersed himself in it and was its greatest supporter within the political system. That included green technologies. Solar, insulators, pumps, batteries, the whole kit. He used it, loved it, and lived by it. Yitzakh certainly saw no conflict; if anything, he saw the Jewish faith as strong for its use of technology. That may include military technology, but he saw it as being wider than that. David had a sling and a river stone to slay Goliath, so we adapt and move with the times, not lay down in the face of our enemies as our sling is shot out of our hands by an AK47.

Israel certainly seemed to have quite a few enemies, so it was a necessity to survive.

Lately, his particular fascination has been with land use. The World Health Organisation has released some very interesting data on the use and availability of arable land. In Israel, they transformed the land from low-grade to arable and made it even better and more productive. So he questioned the World Health Organisation on that, and they changed the documentation to show there may be some land currently listed as barren that can be transformed if nations work together.

Somehow the world needed to give poor African dirt farmers hope, and Yitzakh was sure that Israeli technology and know-how were the answer. Many of those poor African countries had turned to Islam and refused to import Jewish technology on the advice of their more powerful Islamic brother countries. Unfortunately, those brother countries had only come with bank loans and failed advice, making many of those African countries poorer and more desperate.

Today, Yitzakh was going out to visit a few settlements on the edge of the Sinai. Most of the land was once reclaimed, but then much of it was returned as an act of peace. He wasn't sure peace would ever truly come. Given his position, politics was a daily affair, but he tried not to get bogged down in the skirmishes that plagued the region. He wanted a fresh start, not to scratch old wounds. On this excursion Yitzakh was travelling with Daniel, Shira, and Noam. Daniel was Yitzakh's attaché, adviser, and an ordained Rabbi in his own right. Shira and Noam were Yitzakh's security, not that he felt he needed them, but the Rabbinate disagreed. Noam was driving and getting security reports through her bluetooth headset from the *Kibbutz*. Daniel had been trying to get Yitzakh to look through some papers, but Yitzakh didn't like reading in the car. He liked to look out the window, so he didn't miss anything going on outside. Daniel was forcing him to get through the paperwork by reading it to him instead.

"The *Knesset* is proposing that all access to the temple mount be shut down again until the end of Ramadan to stop a repeat of the 2019 outbreak of fighting between the ultra-orthodox and Muslims."

"What does that have to do with me?" Yitzakh hated this bickering.

"You hold the Presidency of the Chief Rabbinate of Israel. They are looking for you to confirm that, from a religious standpoint, such a shutdown of access for both Jews and Muslims will be acceptable to the faithful." Daniel continued.

"Yes, I understand that. But it isn't. It really won't matter what I say." Yitzakh said, not wanting to be dragged into the argument. He saw how it eroded support for his predecessor, and at the time he counselled soft language, but the pressure from the Ultras was too much for his predecessor to bear.

He was not his predecessor. "There is no religious reason for a shutdown of the Temple Mount or the Wailing Wall during Ramadan. We have shared these monuments for more years of peace than years of war. The Prime Minister just likes to poke a stick in the bee hive instead of leaving them to make honey."

"Certainly, that is one point of view," Daniel said warily. "Is that how you would like me to respond?"

"Most certainly not." Yitzakh refused to be drawn into this. "When is my next meeting with Levi?"

Yitzakh would delay and put in a meeting with his Sephardi colleague to try to run down the clock.

"Not scheduled until next week." Daniel said, looking up from his calendar, "The *Knesset* is looking for an answer today."

"Well, *HaShem* works to a timetable, not that of the *Knesset*." Yitzakh puffed himself up. He didn't need to clarify if he wanted to consult.

"The answer will come after that meeting and not before; you can tell them that. Please ensure that is on the agenda for next week's meeting with Levi."

"We could call him now," Daniel said nervously. "We have another..." He looked at Noam for some confirmation of the timing.

"Twenty-five minutes," she replied.

"Twenty-five minutes until we get to the *Kibbutz*," Daniel confirmed.

"Nah." Yitzakh wanted to stretch this out. "Let them stew."

A few minutes went by. Daniel was looking through his papers. Yitzakh was admiring the harsh beauty of the landscape and thinking about the incredible resilience of the people who lived, worked, and maintained these settlements.

"What else do you have?" He queried Daniel.

Daniel could see Yitzakh was not in the mood for anything controversial, so he pivoted to something more personal.

"Most of this is a little overly officious, perhaps saved for a more formal time. Do you mind if I ask you a personal question, perhaps something you might say is part of my learning?"

"Of course, my boy." Yitzakh loved those types of questions.

"If the *Talmud* is clear in lines of words and they have been interpreted so many times over, especially when they pertain to things so commonplace in our society, which in reality remain unchanged through thousands of years, why do you think we seem to get so many requests from the *Knesset* and other secular bodies for interpretation."

Noam took a deep breath from the driver's seat.

"Sorry." Daniel apologised. "It is a long question."

Yitzakh smiled. More for the tone than the length of the question itself.

"Yes," Yitzakh said, taking a moment.

Daniel found Yitzakh very hard to read. Not surprisingly, many other people also did.

"It's OK. I think I see what you're asking." Yitzakh saw an alternative explanation forming in front of him.

"Let's try it this way." He started. "If I ask you if it's raining outside, what answer should I expect?"

Daniel smiled and said, "It's the Sinai. So No"

"So if I ask you again in five minutes, what will the answer be?"

Daniel's smile dulled; he wasn't sure where the joke was going. "Still No."

Yitzakh continued, "So how many times do I need to ask you before you would consider changing that no to a maybe?"

Daniel thought carefully about the answer: "I would assume if it looked like it was going to rain outside. If there were clouds. If I could smell the rain coming,"

Yitzakh encouraged more possibilities. "Yes," he said, "what else might encourage you to give me a maybe?"

"Perhaps if there is a weather report that says it's going to rain." Daniel thought that was a great answer.

"Yes, perfect." Yitzakh got the answer he wanted. "So tell me, Daniel, where does a weather report come from?"

"Well, from the Meteorological Service." Daniel was very sure of his answer.

"Correct!" Yitzakh exclaimed to Daniel who showed visible relief. He even smiled a half smile.

"The Meteorological service possibly gets the information they use to determine the weather from several sources, including very expensive Satellite readings, historical information, and nearby weather stations. I am not 100% sure of where else they get their information, but I know they are not right a lot." Yitzakh said with a big grin. Like he had just proven his point.

"But they are our government's trusted source of all weather information, so we should expect rain if they say so."

Daniel smiled wider, knowing that Yitzakh didn't mean that.

"Better we put our heads out the window or watch the birds and insects, some might say."

"Indeed." Shira piped up from the front passenger seat.

"So, we are the Chief Rabbinate Office," Yitzakh continued. "Equally as historically storied as the Meteorological Bureau," Yitzakh smiled. "Why would we be different?"

He let the thought hang in the air for Daniel to think about. He believed being a good teacher was not about presenting the answers on a plate. It was about getting the student to come to conclusions themselves, with a perspective aligned to a certain vector.

Daniel was trying hard to say that the President of the Chief Rabbinate, Yitzakh, should have been able to answer questions of faith directly. Yitzakh didn't see it that way and knew that the question was not really aimed at faith at all but slanted towards politics. If he answered in any way, then faction leaders, power brokers, and special interest groups would come out of the woodwork looking for a piece of him. But if he held his decision and garnered opinions and trust from special interest groups, then perhaps he would be able to redirect some vectors along the way. Perhaps, just perhaps, a peaceful solution will come to pass. Unlike 2019.

The Range Rover pulled up outside the security gates of the *Kibbutz*. Noam remained behind the wheel, and Shira got out to interface with the security guards. Even the President of the Chief Rabbinate had to allow inspection of the vehicle. This president did it gladly. Noam remained behind the wheel with the engine running in case there was any trouble. Lessons from the past blended into the present to make a better future.

This was Yitzakh's private creed.

His visit was to inspect some of the agricultural technology that the farmers were using. They had invested heavily in technology. Solar pumps and water extractors, heat dissipators, hydroponic monitoring, and robotic weed control, it was all quite amazing. The farm was less like the dusty, ramshackle hovels of the past and more like the Moisture Farm Owen Skywalker had worked at on Tatooine.

Yitzakh had a secondary mission.

He wanted to talk to the local militant ultra-orthodox rabbis that were stirring up trouble in the area and trying to take more land. He had some information that they were the ones behind attempts to close the Temple Mount, stirring up trouble in two places and then using one as a concession for the other. All of this is done by antagonising Muslims. He needed these ultras to stop. They had enough land to farm and live on; even if they said it was their right, they were just being greedy.

What a shame Daniel couldn't see the true purpose of the visit. The boy was smart but still had many years of observation to truly understand the craft of dealing with people for their own good. He was still wanting to grapple with the world head-on. Perhaps after a few hours here he would see; perhaps not.

Yitzakh would not tell him what he was doing; he would need to open his eyes of his own accord.

Yitzakh had no shortage of rabbis. To be honest, he enjoyed keeping himself busy with outings like this, so he wasn't available to create more Rabbis, particularly ultra-orthodox ones. Conservative estimates said that one percent of Israelis were rabbis, which is a lot. A comparison might show Italy had less than one thousandth of one percent of priests and Turkey around the same low percentage of imams. So a trip like this gave Yitzakh the ability to quietly manipulate politics.

That aside, he did love all the gadgets and enjoyed talking to the locals about the blending of faith and technology. It was something other religions just couldn't seem to manage. Maybe some of the Christians had nice websites or used smart boards in their schools, but this was next-level tech.

Nothing short of awesome.

***

The Beautiful Game

Hasan walked around the community centre, pleased to see everything up and running again.

He stopped to talk to some elderly patients and looked in on the nursery.

The director was frantic, as the disruption had seen most parents waiting outside the police barrier with their children in their cars for up to three hours. Many of them just couldn't take the trip home as the traffic was horrendous and they had no one to leave the children with. Many had jobs they were late for, and a few lost those jobs over the incident.

Hasan listened with empathy; he offered to assist those families where he could and set out, with the director, to put together a circular to let them know the whole thing was a massive miscommunication between the Met and the centre. He wanted them to know that the centre management was doing all it could to ensure the same miscommunication was not repeated in the future.

After the meeting with the Childcare director, Hasan was very happy to see an indoor football match being run in the rec centre.

He stayed, watched the game and talked with the rec centre director, who said many of the boys were angry at the treatment by the Met and were discussing ways to retaliate. They were talking about covering up their appearance first; they didn't want to bring shame or heat to the rec centre; just make life sticky for the Met somewhere else.

Hasan silently watched the remainder of the game and listened to the director finish explaining the fallout from this area of the Met's actions.

It was one of his simple pleasures; he loved Football, was a mad Arsenal fan, and dearly loved the rec centre. He pushed them to nurture local talent at the football association level. They currently had seventeen players in all FA competitions, and Hasan kept in contact with all of them. He was proud of those players and of all who could represent the community.

As the game drew to a close, he made his way to the sideline, and when the final whistle blew, he called the boys to his side.

Even if they didn't know him personally, if the imam asks to speak to you, whatever else you have on, you wait to see what he has to say.

"Boys. I have heard some news I need to discuss with you regarding the lockout of the Community centre yesterday by the Metropolitan Police."

A few of the boys grumbled openly, and many looked at their feet.

"The actions of the Met were overzealous and ill-conceived. There is no doubt." Hasan said, raising the volume and tone of his voice to get maximum effect. "But the actions of the Met don't need to encourage us into any form of revenge or payback. We are above that. I am sure you are all capable of concealing your identities to protect the community centre from reprisal." Hasan paused again, looking around at these young men of the future.

"But can you conceal these actions from our Lord Allah or the prophet Muhammad."

He looked out the top window of the gymnasium striking a classic pose to conjure up some of his best improv.

"Our God sees your actions and knows they go against his word. Now, as I have reminded you of this, it also goes against my word."

There is no doubt that among the twenty-six people standing in that circle, more of them would have a greater fear of Hasan than Mohammad or Allah.

Hasan was known for visiting parents, reminding grandparents, and ensuring the whole community knew some things.

Not all things, just things like this.

Allah kept those things quiet.

Hasan had finished speaking, but he remained present to allow his authority to drift back and forth among the boys.

The coach broke the silence, speaking up to reinforce the message.

"Right boys, you heard the imam. Let's put any of those thoughts aside and focus on the matches we have in two days."

The coach clapped his hands three times. "Abyad Akhar, you are travelling to Leyton Orient, so you need to be on the bus at 430 p.m. sharp from bus stop C. Aswad Aşfar. We are hosting Crouch End here at 7 p.m. If you are unsure of the details, check the website or ask."

The coach clapped again three times. "Thanks to the imam for the wisdom of his words."

A general asynchronous chorus clattered around the gym of various praises for the imam.

Hasan felt the message was clear and turned to head back to his office.

His phone let out a familiar ringtone, and as he walked away, he glanced at the sender.

"Message from Yitzakh the Jew"

With the upheaval of the last few days, he had forgotten about the match completely. He didn't need to open the message, as he knew it would say "Spurs 1 Arsenal 0." He had watched the match and knew he would get some communication from the newly elected President of the Chief Rabbinate, who shared Hasan's passion for the round-ball game.

He messaged back to Yitzakh, "Lucky strike. We had 73% possession."

The love of the beautiful game came with its fair share of heartbreaking moments.

A message was returned immediately.

"I saw on the news you have had a few headaches. Need me to put in a good word in the name of interfaith cooperation?"

Hasan allowed himself a chuckle. He could have sent that message to Yitzakh, and the same sentiment would ring true.

The two had met while playing football for their respective schools as kids, and over the course of a single tournament, they realised they lived close together and, religious differences aside, had a lot in common.

So they had become the best of friends.

After college, when Yitzakh left the UK, they stayed in touch and often met at interfaith seminars or on personal trips when protocol would allow.

There was no chance of that now that Yitzakh had risen to the position of President of the Chief Rabbinate.

Who would believe that rough head could rise so high in his faith?

Another message rang out: "Another interfaith brewing in London. I will be there; I hope we can have time to catch up."

Hasan returned to his office and faced another meeting, this time with the waiting director of the Elderly Social Club, which was supposed to be running a well-being club elderly lunch on the day things were shut down. Unfortunately, the caterers had delivered all the food the night before, and so most of the food would soon be spoiled.

"What am I to do, Imam?" Faisal, the senior care director, was not far from being a participant rather than an organiser. "Three hundred covers. All the food will be lost today or tomorrow, as we simply don't have the long-term storage space. Most of the Elderly are now feeling a bit unsure about returning; they are a timid lot who will need some time to forget yesterday's event.

"I agree, Faisal." Hasan saw the timidity of the elderly as the least of all the issues, but he must deal with things on all fronts. "Give me just one moment."

Hasan looked at the contacts directory on his phone; he had placed his phone on the table between himself and Faisal and dialled "Hamza, Muslim Aid."

The phone rang only a single time before Hamza picked up.

"Imam Hasan. *As-Salamu-alaikum.*"

"*Wa-Alikum-asalaam.*" The Imam replied in the traditional greeting and answer. "How are things feeding the hungry, my friend?" The Imam and Hamza had many dealings, so they had a deep familiarity between them. Not friends but trusted colleagues.

"Usual problems, Imam. Too many mouths and not enough food."

"Well Hamza I might just have a solution to get us through today and maybe tomorrow, and from there we will trust in the guidance and blessings of Allah."

"I'm all ears, Imam." Hamza replied optimistically.

"Sitting in front of me is Faisal, our Age Care Director."

"Hello Hamza," Faisal croaked.

"*As-Salam-u-Alaikum*," Hamza replied.

Hasan needed to lead this, so he broke in, "I am sure you heard about our issues here at the Community Centre yesterday. Terrible impact on all facets of our services, all because of three tainted individuals."

"Yes Imam, I heard." Hamza replied. "Shocking business all around. I cannot fathom why they would shut down the whole complex for such a small oversight."

"Indeed." Hasan didn't need to divulge further. "Well, it might be your blessing as we were supposed to have three hundred covers for our age care group annual lunch, which now has had to be cancelled, and we have significant supplies that need to be moved soon or they will spoil. Do you have sufficient storage room for such supplies?"

"Yes, Imam, we can store the goods for you. I have a truck that can collect them from you; I think within an hour, depending on the traffic." Hamza replied.

A favour for the Imam was something well gained, as he would supply a bounty in return.

"Wonderful Hamza. You are truly a man of means, but you misunderstand me. I don't need you to store them for me. I am giving you the supplies as a donation for the needy."

Faisal's face dropped to a frown but quickly changed to a smile when he heard the joy in Hamza's reply.

"Oh, thank you, my imam. What a wonderful gift. I will come in the truck myself to assist."

"Wonderful. Then I will greet you personally when you arrive. See you soon."

"Thank you again, Imam Hasan. See you soon."

As Hasan hung up, a message arrived on his phone from Yitzakh. The name flashed for Faisal to see.

"The Jew!" Faisal almost spat out his teeth. "You are receiving messages from a Jew."

Hasan didn't need to explain himself. Faisal was in no position to question his contacts with other faiths. But Hasan felt the compulsion to stop this pettiness some Muslims had towards Jews in particular.

"Yes, Yitzakh is my lifelong friend. We went to school here in London. He is now the Chief Rabbi of Israel. The two of us share a lifelong love of the most beautiful faith of all."

Faisal just wasn't sure what to say and sat with his mouth open.

"You will catch something if you keep your mouth open that way. COVID-19 or flies, or maybe someone will mistake you for a patron and feed you." Hasan smiled.

"But Imam Hasan. He is a Jew; how can you share faith?" Faisal used the word Jew aggressively and with disdain.

"Football, Faisal. We both love football. He, of course, is a Spurs supporter and so cannot see through both eyes."

Hasan turned and pointed to the various Arsenal memorabilia that decorated his office, teacups, pendants, stress balls, and scarves.

"I am Gunners. So he has been reminding me of the score from yesterday, even though I have other things on my plate and he has others on his."

"It does not reflect well on you to have a Jew as a friend, Imam."

Faisal was old and didn't choose his words carefully, and Hasan knew this, but he had to defend his right to choose his friends.

"No, Faisal, you are wrong. Those attitudes must end. You cannot judge the quality of a man by his faith alone. Yitzakh is a good man, a smart man, a true man, and if you could look beyond your prejudice, maybe you would see that about people from other faiths too."

"Very well, Imam." Faisal knew he had been admonished, and he also knew not to push the Imam.

"But I need to note, Imam." Faisal said. Hasan raised himself in his chair and took a very authoritative stance, ready to remind Faisal who was the Imam.

"A Spurs supporter..."

A twinkle passed in Faisal's eyes as he turned to exit the Imam's office.

"Thank you again, my Imam, for sorting out our problems. You are a man of great wisdom."

Chapter Four

The Mahant

The Shining Student

Maryam was an exemplary student.

Engaged, excellent at recalling facts, very logical, and emotionally intelligent. She took her high-performing memory and applied it skillfully across many tasks. She listened and even took the next step, which so many people miss. She understood. She understood people, and she understood detail.

Maryam was born a Hindu child to parents that were chosen for her according to the karma of her past life. She must have been so good in her past life, as she had wonderful parents. Her parents were kind, thoughtful, hardworking, highly valued, and high-standing members of their community. Maryam, in return, gave thanks to Vishnu and all his avatars. As she grew, she studied Bhakti Yoga under a wonderful swami with the intention of not having worse parents in the next life and following the simple path to the divine. She saw no reason why her path could not combine her faith and her studies.

Applying true dedication to her studies, Maryam was awarded a number of scholarships for her aptitude. From a humble school in the suburbs of Imphal, Manipur, she won a scholarship to the Cambridge School in South Kolkata. From there, a university scholarship to Ashoka University in NCR Dehli and finally a full international scholarship to Cambridge University in the UK.

Her parents were very proud.

Maryam wanted to make a difference in the world, so she studied for a Masters in Engineering for Sustainable Development. The course had so many interesting facets and had lecturers and students who were passionate about the subject. Students at Cambridge were not just traditionally Anglo-Saxon English students. Like Maryam, many students came from abroad or had parents who had come from abroad and settled in the UK.

There was a large mix of many faiths in her class, but she found herself one of only three Hindus, and she was the only Vaishnava, following Vishnu as the supreme manifestation of the divine.

Maryam's time at Cambridge completing her Master's degree was wonderful. She attained the highest marks, and her thesis on the influences of religion on population growth was considered a paper that should be given more time and expanded as part of a doctorate. She was delighted but wanted to expand the topic further.

Maryam undertook a PhD in Future Infrastructure and Built Environment and focused her thesis more on how to create the perfect sustainable society, allowing everyone the right level of resources to achieve maximum potential and, of course, to end human suffering.

It was a mammoth task, including research into the world's energy problems, overcrowding, war, and the human condition globally.

Maryam was given a full scholarship and even backed by a university think tank to expand the horizons of the question.

Her doctoral supervisor was a brilliant professor, considered at the forefront of his field. Maryam worked very hard on the doctorate programme, tutored as many classes as she could, and found some social time to spend with her parents and university friends to keep her life in balance. She continued her Bhakti Yoga with a swami from the theology faculty at Cambridge and felt her life in perfect harmony.

Her only vice was a feeling that things were so good because she tried and worked so hard, which may have been more of a truism and might lead her to narcissism.

She often discussed her PhD work with her Bhakti Yoga swami over lunch that she would prepare for him, which they would share on the beautiful grounds at Cambridge.

The long, slow development of her thesis had many religious aspects. The swami was most interested; he himself participated in many interfaith meetings and had a wider knowledge of other faiths.

After many such lunches and over many months, the swami asked if Maryam would mind meeting the head of the Hindu faith in the UK and explaining more of her thesis to him. The swami had shared some of the content with the Mahant at BAPS Shri Swaminarayan Mandir, the largest Hindu temple in London, and he had shown great interest in her topic, and in Maryam.

***

The Man Makes The Moment

Mahant Swami Muktananda was a very astute man.

In 2012, he was anointed as the future spiritual and administrative leader of the Hindu faith in the UK by Paramahamsa Swami Maharaj, his predecessor.

With the passing of Paramahamsa Swami Maharaj in 2016, he assumed the role with vigour.

The first thing he noticed was that faith was in decline. He was further saddened when he discovered this was not just in the UK, but globally. His sadness turned to abject grief when he met other faith leaders and found that most other faiths were suffering similar declines.

What to do?

He trusted the members of his group in the UK, so he put out a message to them to look for ways we could best combat this trend. If need be, he counselled, they must think outside the proverbial *Diwali* trinket box.

Some responses were well-meaning but impossible. Like the *Pandit* in Cornwall who suggested that money be given out during morning and afternoon prayer, surely that will bring the faithful in. He also laughed when another *pujari* suggested that all prayer should be moved from the home to the temple to encourage membership.

"How would they stop people from praying in their homes?" he pondered.

His email wasn't bogged down with suggestions, so when he received a message from the swami at Cambridge University, he knew, in his bones and in his soul, that this solution was worth pursuing. One of the brightest of all stars among the Indian students in England was in her final PhD year and had developed a thesis to end human suffering. Finally something that could unite the faithful.

Mahant Swami Muktananda, like many other leading theologians, knew that faith was not disappearing.

Faith simply doesn't work that way.

The faith organisations of the world were just being undermined.

In the past, it had been done by the government, using faith when it suited self-interest and discarding it or chastising the temples when it didn't. There was no doubt in Mahant Swami Muktananda's mind that he could smell the hand of the government in much of this. But it seemed to him that so many governments had been hijacked by the green movement, a faith pretending to be a science.

Led by the worst of them, the angry dwarf Greta.

She seemed angry at everything.

Maybe with the help of rational, intelligent minds free of history, like Maryam, they could fight fire with fire and recapture the hearts of the faithful. He knew there was an interfaith meeting coming up. The bishop in Oxford had given this one a code name: Banding together to tackle the false green faith. According to the bishop, the whole Christian group felt they needed the Hindus to be part of a strong alliance to make this work.

It was especially required as they were likely to get no support from the Muslims.

The Mahant laughed. At first, he thought maybe the green movement was for Muslims. No doubt, the Christians and the Muslims had histories, as did the Hindus and the Muslims, and he supposed similarly did the Christians and the Hindus.

The bishop had asked if the Mahant would be able to find a notable speaker, as they had reserved a speaking place for the Hindu contingent. She had been clear that King Charles would make an opening address and the Dalai Lama would provide an address first on day two. She was hoping he could come up with something special for the remainder of day two. Apparently, day three was currently earmarked for a Muslim speaker and an American marketing expert who was more of a motivational speaker than anything else.

Go out with a bang, the bishop had said.

Did she mean the Muslim speaker, the Mahant chuckled to himself.

The bishop's theories were sound and very much aligned with his own research since taking on his role. Somehow he needed to find consensus amongst his brethren. They were a difficult lot to inspire, and as a general rule, they didn't like change. They certainly didn't want anything to change anything they were currently working through.

Some of them had been working on those things internally and spiritually for decades.

The Mahant put out a message to all the heads of the UK council. He made it simple: they would meet twice, the first time to be introduced to Maryam and see a presentation of her work. Each council member, if unable to make any decision on behalf of their group, would have one week to return their decision at a follow up meeting. He simply didn't have time to wait for a guru on a rock to see a sparrow fleeing a ravenous hawk for a decision to be ratified.

Consult your deity and decide; no dilly-dallying.

If they could get a majority without any dissenters, Maryam would take the podium at the interfaith conference and present her thesis with the blessing of the Hindu council.

The Mahant needed a meeting room away from the usual Hindu business to conduct this special presentation.

Hindus were a very community-based people, generally speaking, so having anything like a private meeting for any length of time was virtually impossible in or near any temple or community hall.

Interruptions for tea, food, news, family, decisions to be made as part of other councils, clearing away, tidying up, then more tea, and then more food, brought constant unwanted interruptions.

He needed focus, so he booked a meeting room in Chelsea, hopefully far enough away from any temple. He arranged all the food, ensuring all dietary variations were catered for, and he paid. He even arranged for drivers to pick up the council members from their local temples so they wouldn't need to bring an entourage.

Each council member was allowed just one adviser. The meeting would consist of two one-hour sessions with a break in between when phone calls and other business could be dealt with, but no one was permitted to leave the meeting. If they left they wouldn't be permitted reentry and he would cast their vote.

When he first assumed his position, the Mahant could not believe how much like herding cats the council meetings were. People not involved in council business would wander in and out with plates of food, drinks, messages, laptops, and newspapers.

It was like a tube station.

Many of the council members spoke dialects from their homeland, which in the majority were Hindi but also ranged to Gujarati, Tamil, Kannada, Bengali, Oriya, Telugu, Marathi, Rajasthani, Nepali, Sinhala, and Maithili. The council only had fifteen members, but in general, only twelve turned up at any one time, some would come late, others would leave early.

The meetings could sometimes have fifty people in them: entourage, onlookers, drivers, brothers, cousins, and, less often than not, council members might bring someone religious.

Part of the problem was that meetings were four hours long with no breaks; that was his first change.

Meetings became just one hour on, thirty minutes off, one hour on, thirty minutes off, and one last hour. There was no smoking, no food, and no phones during the contact hours. He allowed tea and water, which were provided in the room, to be drunk.

He allowed one advisor to sit with each councillor, and they could only confer on or off-record in English or Hindi.

He made all council meetings follow a strict tabled agenda and recorded every-thing.

What a change.

Chaos still prevailed more often than not, but some things slipped through the cracks and actually got done.

Hindu people are well-educated, enthusiastic, and hard-working, but they do like to discuss things. Some might say they like to discuss a little too much.

Being in the UK for a while has made many of them rich, and many of them have considered that money gives their voice more weight.

More money, more to say.

The Mahant tried to modify that practice by realigning the council members with the temples and the population. He made it more about Hinduism and less about self-interest.

It wasn't the Indian business council; it was the Hindu council.

This didn't make him popular, but it did gain some order and help to better align the four major denominations of Hinduism: Vaishnavism, Shaivism, Shaktism, and Smartism.

He reset the council to allow two members from each faction, spread over the temples in the two main geographic areas of London and Leicester.

To give everyone access, he arranged it so that other members could submit a petition to the council through his office. If things fell to a deadlock in meetings, having an even number of other members left him to cast the deciding vote.

One might consider a divine hand in the council's transformation leading up to this decision, but the Mahant just thought it was good organisation.

***

Always Putting Your Best Foot Forward

Maryam strode confidently into the meeting room.

She was prepared, polished, and punctual; what more could she be?

She had not met any of the members of the Hindu Council in the UK, just the Mahant. Her own Cambridge Scholars, who weren't part of the council, were attending today to assist her should she need it. She felt confident she would not, but she always appreciated the support of her community.

The council meeting had already been running for an hour. All of the council's time was taken up discussing the interfaith meeting. Without the Mahant's knowledge, many of the UK-based factions had organised some international guests. They included BK Shivani, Osho, and Sadguru Jaggi Vasudev, who were celebrities on a par with the Dalai Lama in India. There was a fierce debate transpiring, arguing that one of them should be speaking on behalf of Hinduism, not this girl.

But the Mahant held true to his original plan and turned the meeting around. They would listen to Maryam, and if they reached a majority without any dissenters, they would proceed. The whole conversation was taken in front of her, like she was yet to be visible.

Putting the last hour aside and existing in the moment, Maryam began to speak, beginning with her own life in a descriptive but concise format. Within a few minutes, she moved on to faith, her devotion to Vishnu, her study of Bhakti Yoga, and the support of her mentor at the university, with a nod to her swami, who was sitting proudly on the outer.

Maryam outlined her PhD abstract and tried to explain to the council that what she was presenting was a dot-point version. She tactfully added that the presentation has been reduced in size and difficulty to allow the audience to better digest its complexity.

Maryam waited for any feedback. The large man in the corner of the table with a large sign in front of him saying "Emeritus Professor Doctor Patel" coughed slightly. Less to pass any infection or to relieve this throat as to voice his presence and perhaps his intellect.

Maryam took the silence from the rest of the room as a sign she could move on. She started with a summary of her abstract.

Abstract

Creating the perfect sustainable society.
Allowing everyone the right level of resources
to achieve maximum potential and provide a
pathway to end human suffering.

She stopped long enough for the slowest of readers to complete the sentence.

"My initial aim was not to promote any faith," she elaborated, "just to try to outline a fairer world where resources are better shared to allow people to be more useful and subsequently more fulfilled."

She waited for any questions.

A small, wiry, very dark man cleared his throat. "Yes." He said deeply "Narendra Mathur from the Shree Temple in Leicester."

"Yes, sir," Maryam replied respectfully, "your question."

"I will keep it short." He shot a look at the Mahant, wary that the clock was ticking. "If you are not promoting the faith, and by that, I am assuming that is the Hindu faith in general and not any other faith, then why, my dear, with all due respect, are we expected to give up our only speaking slot at an interfaith conference when we have such shining lights as Osho attending who will speak of the faith and the path like it is the air we breathe and the sun that shines?"

"Shivani would make a better speaker." A bald man stood up to add his two cents.

Many others went to speak, but the Mahant raised his hand, and the room fell silent.

"Let's allow Maryam to continue and not call into question her devotion or her suitability just yet."

The room fell silent. Maryam quickly moved to the second slide.

Education

Better Education through lower class sizes, more funding and a greater emphasis on teachers as educators.
- Smaller class sizes will alleviate teachers from being in essence crowd control and allow them to focus on education
- Smaller class sizes allow an emphasis on streamlining student strengths and weaknesses, ensuring graduated students are more productive and useful to society
- Better-educated people are less likely to commit petty crimes
- Money saved on policing could be redirected to education
- More teachers would mean lower unemployment
- Better education increases innovation
- Zones with higher innovation solve more problems around water, housing, hygiene, disease and food production

She spoke freely over the top of the slides. She didn't read them to her audience, as both she and they were intelligent people. She spoke passionately and knowledgeably. "My own experience," she detailed, "was of a nothing girl from a poor Hindu area, cared for by her teachers, embraced by her community, and now educated to the highest level, returning the investment in myself in an innovative way."

Emeritus Professor Doctor Patel puffed out his chest; he knew education was the key.

With a sideways look at the Mahant, a well-built, very handsome older man raised his beautiful baritone voice. "Are you suggesting there should be no police?"

"No, sir," Maryam clarified, "policing will always be needed for community service and law enforcement. The suggestion is just that lower crime rates will mean a smaller police footprint. My thesis explains this in full with examples like Finland, Denmark, and Latvia, which have the lowest police footprints matched with low-class sizes, high education values, and low petty crime rates."

Maryam waited a moment to see if the handsome older man wanted to add anything else.

She rounded out her statement. "The mathematics of those three metrics hold true from the smallest countries to the largest."

The handsome man nodded his approval.

Maryam moved on to the next slide again going into detail and speaking passionately.

Sustainability

For the sustainability of Humanity
- Population density & distribution
- Wilderness allocation
- Water availability focus (not damming) based on human need and grey water recovery
- Open space and air recycling
- Fallow land and future habitation

"The population of the earth is almost eight billion people. According to the World Health Organisation, there is more than enough arable land for double that number of people. The problem is that much of that arable land is in the hands of people who choose not to work it or allow it to be worked. The WHO also stipulates that there is a perfect ratio of arable land to wilderness allocation that allows the recycling of carbon dioxide, allowing fresh air for all.

The Emeritus Professor couldn't hold himself back. "What do you mean no damming?" he burst out. The Mahant gave him a look, reminding him that he should wait for questions at the end.

"Yes, sir." Maryam said. "Dams are causing problems in our riverways, international problems. The Chinese dammed the Mekong River upstream, which caused entire villages that have lived a river life in Cambodia for centuries to have no water.

These poor people were neither consulted nor compensated.

Rivers spread nutrients and topsoil, and break up rocks, mountains, and glaciers. Blocking them causes huge detrimental effects to our landscapes."

"But we need the water," the professor continued his argument.

"Indeed we do, sir." Maryam agreed. "But should we be damming to collect water for hydroelectricity at the detriment of the renewal of the landscape? There are other solutions like atmospheric condensation, desalination, rainwater collection, and as a last resort, localised artesian bores. Much of the infrastructure around dams has been about centralising control of water resources by governments without proper consideration of the impact."

The professor nodded, not so much at the content as at the clarity of the argument. He noted to himself that he should read her paper.

The Mahant smiled, maybe she would win the room one heart at a time.

Maryam continued, and the room went silent as people listened, enchanted by Maryam's mix of intelligence, empathy, and social grace.

Infrastructure

Infrastructure and demographics of populations
- Place population around water and food sources to minimise transport overheads on resources.
- Restricted leisure travel based on a distance-based sustainable travel credit scheme
- Implement available technology improvements in resource usage and recycling

Maryam spoke passionately of the burden that transport was placing on the world's resources.

Mostly in the name of greed.

"Why are we eating Brazilian grapes in the winter in the UK?"

"Why do we need to fly to Mexico to sit on a beach?"

"Our local producers are selling goods to global markets, while our local market is buying from global producers."

"The transport cost seems low per item, but the cost to the community and the planet is devastating."

Maryam barely raised her voice but managed to convey passion through gravitas. "Our eating habits, our travel habits, and our localisation of resources do not match our infrastructure or our capabilities. Most of the reasons we are developing these habits are for greed."

She waited to see the reaction, and without any word, she continued. "Greed fed by global trade, 'I can't make enough money for my Ferrari F25 by selling to my district, so I will sell to the rest of the UK. That's going well; let's add France and Spain. Oh, now I want a family holiday to the Whitsundays in Australia to see the Great Barrier Reef, so I will sell to America, Canada, and India to increase my sales'."

She paused, a short punctuated moment.

"Such madness must end."

Maryam took a rejuvenating breath.

"According to recent studies, eighty percent of the world's population relies on imported food. Some of that has been due to conflict, but a lot of it is due to consumption habits which are not sustainable.

Importing grain from a summer country in the winter is not sustainable. Grains must be stored in the summer for the harder months ahead, not sold for profit by greedy individuals, only for others to then have to purchase them again from another source.

We must look to turn around the eighty percent and get back to local produce."

No one in the room was going to disagree with that logic, even if they did like Brazilian grapes.

Population Reduction

Population Reduction
- Better redefine incentivised wealth equalisation
- Innovate to care better for the elderly and disabled
- Immediate population reduction through birth control/licensing
- Long-term sustainable controls put in place

Possible controls

Zero Population Growth → Everyone can have two children without penalty which is Zero Population Growth

Removal of Genetic Imperfections → An exclusion by medical/genetic grounds is possible. People with known genetic problems will not be permitted a birth child. They can adopt if capable of caring

Birth License → Everyone must pre-purchase the minimum amount of land a human needs to be productive for thier child. You must also purchase a carbon allocation/wilderness land. This can be a group of trees in a forest which cannot be cut down as it is to keep people on the planet alive.

Community Support → Additional government/community support will be available for people who don't have children as they age

After a change of slide the room lit up.

Everyone was talking at once.

Maryam stood quietly; there was no doubt this was the most controversial of her topics, and some would say the most necessary. It was the elephant in the room, and Maryam said a small silent prayer to Ganesh, the remover of obstacles, to deliver her through this. The Mahant also knew this would not go down well.

As was his will, he stood and, in his normal voice, just said "Gentlemen."

He waited, not in the habit of saying such things twice, for the room to calm, and it did.

"This is a controversial topic, and Maryam and I have discussed its inclusion. We all know that, as a religion, we Hindus promote no ban on birth control. We know some of our own scriptures include advice on what a couple should do to promote conception, and we provide contraceptive advice to those who want it. Our stance is clear." He raised himself up slightly to excentuate the point with his body language.

"This slide, this document Maryam has produced, just puts that in perspective globally. China is already travelling well down this path, and we can see that it is clearly needed in Africa and, to an extent, in India. Overpopulation causes many localised social issues, and this is merely one way to address such issues. Let's try to keep perspective; we have just a little time left. Maryam, you may continue."

Maryam was a little in awe. The Mahant was a nice man to have on your side in an argument.

She flipped to the final slide.

Implement Social Changes

- Army and Sovereignty – The use of resources for armaments is minimised
- Language and culture – A long path to minimise diversity in language and culture
- Religion and diversity – A single Monotheistic faith with other deities reduced to demi-gods. The name of God within the faith setting is not as important as showing faith. This will lead to fewer resources wasted on multiple denomination schools, hospitals and places of worship
- Corruption and crime – The implementation of better education followed by harsher penalties for repeat offence including state-administered death and incarceration

Maryam spoke slowly regarding the devastation of war on the world.

For those like her, who were lucky enough not to have been directly affected, the constant barrage of news on Ukraine, The Middle East, Myanmar, Ethiopia, and more, showed enough of its effect. The statistical detail associated with those wars and many others showed that they were bad for every single metric. Without doubt they were overwhelmingly the most direct cause of human suffering, not just for combatants and regional civilians, but globally. She moved over the need to build bridges in humanity, not separate ourselves through culture and language.

If Hindus could lead the charge, not by dropping our mother tongues but by a compulsory adoption of another language or two, it would help the world be subject to less such conflict. If Mandarin, French, and English were taught alongside your mother tongue and your neighbour's tongue, this may go a long way towards solving conflicts. She added that there must be a reason Switzerland and Botswana can stay peaceful through the ages.

The man, who had remained silent to date, spoke up, looking to stare down Maryam disrespectfully.

"You said you were Vaishnava, didn't you, Maryam?"

"Yes, sir, I try to follow the four regulative principles," Maryam replied proudly.

The man returned to his silence, but his point was made.

Maryam finished up her speaking quickly, as she was mindful that her allotted time was running out. She covered the allocation of resources around schools, hospitals, and care facilities, not to mention places of worship. All were replicated, allowing only the members of that faith to utilise those facilities, while others went without or built likewise underutilised facilities.

She clarified how this could be different if one amalgamated faith was adopted.

It didn't have to change who anyone prayed to, and it would help facilities be better maintained for a mixed-faith congregation. People could pray to whatever God they chose, but the doctrine would slowly be consolidated to use words that were less Hindu, less Christian, and less Islamic and covered more of the combined principles of all faiths.

All faiths had so many common threads seemingly wrapped in different paper.

Before any further discussion transpired, the Mahant raised a finger to Maryam to indicate it was time.

He rose from his chair and addressed the room. He could feel the spike rising from the last comment.

"Gentlemen, please thank Maryam for her presentation. We have run out of our allocated time, so we must cut it short there. I am sure you can all get a picture of her presentation, and like me, you can see that Maryam is a very charismatic and authentic public speaker. Perhaps different than the other proposed choices, but I think showing Hinduism leading the way to the future."

The Mahant himself was very sure this was the best presentation for the interfaith meeting. He had seen the other speakers before, either in person or on video. They asked questions rather than providing answers or provided answers that were further questions. This girl was putting it out there, raw. Here's what's wrong with our world, do we have the strength to take it on?

Did they?

He thought about the Hindu attitude towards birth control.

There was nothing in the *Veda* about birth control, certainly no ban on it. There is nothing in the Quran or the Buddhist Scriptures either, but the Catholics always go in to bat for the fact that there will be no birth control.

As a man of strategy and gamesmanship, he looked forward to the Catholics versus the rest of the world to see how things would fall.

Chapter Five

The Cardinal

Time doth transfix

Victor was a master problem-solver.

That was not why this became his problem; he had a closer tie to this one. The Catholic Church was beset by more than its fair share of scandals.

As a man of action, Victor would never see an end to them.

This scandal had made its way to the College of Cardinals. It wasn't the first scandal to reach those hallowed doors, but the George Pell outcome didn't tarnish the office as much as it did the man. This one is likely to go just that step further, as they all did. Was no one in the church happy with being caught holding hands in the park anymore?

As the Pope explained the details of this scandal, you could see the tears in his eyes, his voice shaking as each word fell, and his emotions on display as the office he had given his life to nurture and grow was to be singed to the core and burned to the ground by the folly of a weak man.

As Victor had led the calls to His Holiness for Bishop Weber to be elevated, His Holiness had given Victor the solemn task of handling Cardinal Weber's indiscretions.

His Holiness had not offered Cardinal Weber a lifeline, unlike George Pell, and that in itself was a damning indictment of his guilt.

Victor's ears may have also curled as the Pope listed off the facts and showed him the evidence in the form of photographs, receipts, ticket stubs, and invoices. Photographs so damning in the arrangement of bodies and equipment, unimpeded by shaky operation. Photographs that were so clearly taken by a couple in a moment, a moment that would drive a stake through the heart of the Vatican.

"We must be ready to act if these ever reach the light of day." The Pope was clear. "We will not jump, but we will be ready should someone push."

"Yes, Your Holiness. Can I confirm they were consenting adults? The young lady... can I say that? The young one doesn't look so very young, less like the problems we have had in the past with other brethren."

"Time doth transfix the flourish set on youth and delves the parallels in beauty's brow." The Pope quoted so eloquently.

"Your Holiness, your wisdom extends to all things." Victor was amazed that, at 86 years old, the Pope could still recall Shakespeare in English.

He had been and was still a remarkable man.

"These things and others you must find out subtly and with extreme discretion, Victor. Trust no one, not even those in the Vatican. This place is the world's largest pasta colander." The Pope cast his gaze around the cherished walls of his private chapel.

"As you wish your holiness. May I first ask the origins of these documents?"

"They were delivered to the Papal Office by courier and opened by the Secretary of State himself as they were marked private to me. He bought them for me directly, and on my orders, he has already paid the demands. The negatives and original SD card were couriered soon after. No one has seen them except myself."

The Pope took a moment, crossed himself, and looked skyward for strength.

"The Secretary of State and yourself. We are hoping it was the young one who made the demands and there are no further copies, but we are not sure." The Pope was visibly shaken.

"Please, Papa, take a chair." Victor was only eight years younger, but the last few years had been hard on his holiness with Pell and then the Ukraine War. His age was showing.

The Pope sat down and took a deep breath. Constricted, he took another.

"Thank you, my friend."

"I will begin with a stern talk to Cardinal Weber and move quickly to secure the details of the young one. From there, we can see what damage control is needed. I will personally prepare press releases and papal responses should this break in the press. If you can muster the strength, Papa, I will report twice weekly or more urgently should I need to."

The Pope folded his fingers across Victor's hand and grasped it in a single motion of gratitude.

"You have my warmest thanks and my prayers until we can have better news."

The sadness in the Pope's voice would melt the coldest heart.

"As always, you are the only one I can trust with such delicate things. Hopefully, we will take these things to our grave to spare the world such depravity."

"I am afraid the world already gets its fair share of depravity, your holiness. Such pictures and videos are commonplace and open on the Internet."

The Pope looked forlornly at Victor as a tear blossomed and faded into the wizened well of his eyes, and with his voice unable to confirm or deny, his head nodded in silent regret.

"I also have the interfaith conference on the decline of religions worldwide at the hands of the green movement. The Anglican Bishop says they are stealing the faithful from our pews, and we must act. She has a plan for an interfaith collective of some kind."

"Yes, Victor. I know you will represent us well. You are a master at such things. We can talk about the outcomes on your return from London. But this matter, must take precedence."

"Yes, Your Holiness, as you wish."

Victor made his exit, leaving the Pope to ponder his regrets.

As the Cardinal who presides over the Apostolic Chamber and a member of the Commission of Cardinals for the Vatican Bank, Victor was indisputably the most powerful member of the College of Cardinals and a successor in waiting for the Pope. He was often given these difficult tasks because he had something greater than power and influence.

He had the trust of the Pontiff.

Something he earned and would not swap for a million villas in Tuscany.

He made his way down the long corridor that linked the Apostolic Palace and the Roman Curia offices. With each step, more thoughts sprang to Victor's mind, other disturbing breaches of trust that the clergy had subjected the faithful to. This young one, even though an abomination in the eyes of many Catholics, was still to be treated as a trusted member of the flock.

A member whose trust had been breached by someone who should know better.

Victor had the cell phone number of Bishop Weber. The two of them had a long history together; maybe that was part of Victor's surprise at all this.

Bishop Weber had never mentioned to him any carnal thoughts. In all their years rising through the ranks of the Church, they never mentioned any burning passions except for the scriptures, Mary the Mother of Christ, and the Holy Sepulchre.

Anyway, to action.

That was Victor.

"Martin, where are you at the moment?" Victor didn't mince words.

"Victor, how are you?" Bishop Weber was generally a friendly guy. Perhaps Victor never guessed quite how friendly.

"Good Martin. I have lots on and was hoping we could catch up for a coffee, lunch, or something. Are you in the Vatican or out on your travels still?"

"I just flew out of Bangkok after a week with Michael the Archbishop, going over some curriculum adjustments to try and keep the Thai government-mandated global warming rubbish from swamping our Catholic teaching of earth sciences. Currently in transit in Dubai, I will be back in Europe tomorrow. I am scheduled to fly into Frankfurt, but I might take a train home for the weekend. I don't need to be in the Vatican until Monday. Can it wait until after that?"

Victor knew it couldn't; the candle was burning.

"How about I meet you at that super stylish fish restaurant on the lake tomorrow for lunch?" Victor was deliberately non-committal.

"Great." Martin's voice was a little shaky. "Everything OK, Victor?"

"Yes, I just need a bit of one-on-one, like in the old days, face-to-face, heart-to-heart."

Everyone in the Vatican knew Victor asked the questions that the Pope wouldn't ask for himself; no one would say no, but Victor was an old friend too, keeping it close to his chest.

"It would be wonderful to see you again; how long has it been?" Martin was trying to be friendly; Victor appreciated it but needed to keep it brief.

"At least a year, I think. I have another call, Martin. I will see you there at noon. I will get my office to arrange it all. OK?"

"Great yes." Martin's voice trailed off as Victor put the phone on the desk and hung up. There was no other call, and he said a hail Mary for this smallest of white lies.

Tomorrow.

Victor checked his calendar. He had a number of calls during the morning that he could easily take on the train; he would need a private carriage, so he immediately sent an email out to his secretary to get the train booked there in the morning from Milan and back, leaving around four in the afternoon. He could head to Milan by plane tonight to get a head start.

His phone buzzed, and he received a voicemail notification.

He dialled the voicemail and put the phone on speaker, still on the desk.

"Cardinal, this is the bishop of Oxford. I am calling regarding the interfaith meeting next week in London. I'm just confirming you will be attending and hoping you have some names of the other attendees from the Catholic contingent. There are no limitations from our point of view, as we have booked a large auditorium. We have a couple of key speakers. King Charles, the Dalai Lama, and some motivational speaking from Marcus Davenport. We also have a presentation from the Hindu contingent, who will show us one possible path that will allow us to claim faith back from those terrible green impostors."

Victor was well aware of the interfaith conference, and he had hand-picked his team. He saw this as a great chance to expand the Catholic message. There is a possibility that this was what Victor was put here on the planet for, his great aria in God's opera.

He had arranged a crack team of cardinals and bishops from Indonesia, the Philippines, Sudan, Pakistan, Thailand, and a large contingent from the US who could argue cultural issues with other faiths. He backed them up with ordained legal teams who understood religious laws from about half the countries on earth and, with all due respect, all the important ones. He had already had numerous conversations with the bishop of Oxford. Surprisingly, they had found common ground on many issues. Mostly, they talked about the effect of the new cultural revolution on the church, particularly that of the greens but also the LGBTQ+ community, women's groups, and academics.

Personally, the academics hurt Victor the most. Studies showed that in some regions, 97% of academics were not religious and considered all religion to be for the poor and stupid. In other cases, they had teamed up with the greens to show scientific proofs of things the religious organisations had always asked people to take on faith.

He laughed to himself as he thought of Douglas Adams words. "For an encore, man goes on to prove that black is white and gets himself killed on the next zebra crossing."

Anyway, if the religions of the world could find a way to band together to tackle the problem head-on, he wanted to be there in the vanguard, as prepared as he could possibly be.

He made a note to include the cardinal of Vietnam, as now he might not be able to bring the cardinal of Thailand. They both had a great rapport with the Buddhist group, so either would do, and if both were there, we would truly have the Buddhists on our side.

He knew the Catholics would be important in these discussions; holding the largest percentage of faithful helped, but the truth is they also held the key to it all: the bankroll. The only groups with anywhere near enough money, the

Jews and the Scientologists, were unlikely to go with it. It would be best for the mother church to be there as a shoulder for the other faiths to lean on.

He put in a call to Jessica and smiled to himself at the babelfish in those hilarious Adams books.

A dead giveaway. Wonderful.

"This is Jessica, Bishop of Oxford. I'm not currently available to take this call. Please leave a short message including your number, and I will return your call when I am first available."

Voicemail.

Victor hated voicemail. He hated his own, and he hated other people's. It was wrong to hate, but in the case of voicemail, he would take absolution later.

"Ciao Jessica" Victor was deliberately informal. "Victor from the Vatican. Yes, we are one hundred percent for the Interfaith Meeting in London. We come to listen, and with the blessing of the Papa, we come to participate. We will have fifty of our keenest minds in our group. I have confirmation from most and some others on standby in case they can't make it. In the worst-case scenario, I will pull in some additional Catholics from the UK if the airlines let us down. I am sure you appreciate that, from my end, it's a large undertaking. You have my number if you need to discuss it further. If not, I look forward to seeing you on Wednesday. Maybe we can organise a side meeting between our two faiths, as friends in God."

Victor hung up and went to his private quarters to prepare for his journey to talk to Bishop Webber. He had three other meetings that afternoon before Vespers and would then take a late flight to Milan, where he would stay in a suite provided by the Archdiocese.

***

Later that night in Milan, the sky was clear and bright; the stars that rang so clearly from his home balcony in Tuscany were starkly absent from the skies here.

Victor missed the majesty of those stars.

The way the Milky Way webbed its way across the sky, dotted with the brightest stars shining out the message of the glory of God, In Milan, a dull sky presented itself in comparison. If one were to believe the scientific explanation, it was because the pollution didn't allow the stars above to shine through.

Victor wasn't convinced.

He had read texts from the Vatican library about the glory of the stars above Milan from scholars past. They had even sketched the beautiful arches formed in the sky and the heavenly chandeliers that decked those arches in a majesty that can only be wondered at and never denied.

Milan had always had pollution, and it's true that things in these modern times are different, but Victor suspected it was something more sinister.

Victor crossed himself as a cold chill passed over his body and took to his bed for the night.

***

The Cardinal Sin

The train ride north was uneventful, thankfully.

Most trains out of Italy are on time, clean, and free of problems. But according to the terms and conditions on the reverse side of the ticket, there is no guarantee.

Victor had left early to make the lakeside restaurant with plenty of time to spare, and he arrived at eleven thirty as scheduled. He was picked up by a local car provided by the diocese. In this case, it was a large BMW 7 Series, which was spacious and luxurious and powerful without compromise. There was some simplicity in travelling as a Cardinal, especially a very high-ranking Cardinal. First, Victor still had relative anonymity. If the Pope tried to travel like this, he would be mobbed or worse. But best of all, he had influence.

One call from either of his travel staff would have a car there to pick him up, sometimes with a small entourage, but generally, he would say, no fuss, so there would just be a driver. Victor found that less fuss meant he got more done, but sometimes fuss was an occupational hazard.

The restaurant was, as he recalled, nestled on a beautiful, sweeping promontory, curving its way around the coast, giving each diner a full view of the lake and the mountains behind it in all their glory. The lake was sparkling, and the clarity of the backdrop provided a sense of awe against the vivid blue of the lake. He marvelled at God's glory and crossed himself in thanks.

Victor was early, but he had arranged for the private suite to be booked, and he was immediately shown through to be seated. He ordered an espresso and waited patiently, the view holding him tightly in an intense exaltation of mind and feelings.

The coffee arrived, along with a note.

He opened the note, a message from Martin.

"My apologies, Victor. I am running about 15 minutes late. Please order if you are hungry, and I will join you soon. M."

Victor detested tardiness. There was no reason or excuse.

Was his time so unimportant? He had just travelled for hours to be here; Martin had only to travel twenty-five minutes, and yet he could not be on time.

He sat back and was again enthralled by the view. It really did leave him speechless.

Victor reached down and took a sip of the espresso.

"Oh, saints be praised!" he thought. The coffee was exquisite. Elegant, noble, sensual, clean, true, and refined. He closed his eyes and allowed the sense of chocolate, flowers, fruit, and toasted fragrances to drift over him. The sensation drew on for a few seconds and into a blissful minute.

"*Perfetto*," Victor said out loud.

"Can I assist your eminence?" A voice came from behind him.

Victor hadn't noticed that a waiter was standing ready to serve in the corner of the room.

"Oh, my apologies, my son, I did not see you there; perhaps I was so enraptured by this view." Victor had no reason to make excuses for himself. "I just commented to myself on the quality of your espresso. It is truly uplifting to my very soul."

Victor turned to face the waiter, a tall, skinny man, and gave a swirl of his hand.

"*Complimenti.*" he added in his native Italian.

"Thank You, Your Eminence. I will pass your compliments to our barista."

"*Grazie.*" Victor returned to the view and was again lost for a moment in the splendour and the coffee.

Martin rushed through the door, not waiting for it to be opened by the maitre'd, who was trying to give his very best service. He didn't see such high-ranking clergy often but wanted to encourage them to visit more.

"Victor, my old friend. It's been too long." Martin embraced Victor, and Victor returned the embrace warmly.

"Martin, you look great. You must be travelling well at your age." At heart, even though Victor had difficult business to discuss, the two were old and good friends.

"Thank you, my friend. I found a new lease on life travelling in Asia. The cities are so full of chaos and life. Maybe the Italian in you can understand." Martin smiled joyfully.

"Yes, but maybe not." Victor didn't want to agree too much with that statement.

"I have just had the most amazing espresso. Should we make an order? I find myself a little hungry after the long journey from Milan."

"You came from Milan, not the Holy City?" Martin enquired.

"I spent the night in Milan to ease the trip. My presence is not required in the Vatican every night."

"Right." Martin was relieved. "Sorry, I was late. I took the liberty of calling ahead to the restaurant and ordering in advance for us. Some *Mozzarella di Bufala Arancini, Kumara Ravioli, Gamberi alla Busara*, and the fish of the day, which I understand is perch pan-fried and accompanied by an *insalata di finocchi e arance.*"

"Wonderful Martin." Victor knew that Martin wasn't a complete flake. It was good to see he hadn't entirely forgotten his friend.

Martin turned to the waiter. "Can I add a New Zealand Sauvignon Blanc to go with the meal and some still and sparkling Perrier?"

He turned back to Victor and asked, "Anything else, your eminence?" he smiled.

"No, thank you; that all sounds *fantastico*." Victor also smiled back warmly.

The drinks were delivered immediately, and the *arancini* soon after.

Victor took some time just to chat with Martin and didn't head straight to business. The two talked through some Vatican politics, a bit of spiritual theorising, and even some world affairs. The meal was fragrant and elegant but also had an element of the wholesome; it was not like *Nona* was cooking in the kitchen but perhaps was supervising from a stool in the corner.

As the second hour passed and the meal was done, Victor suggested a small digestive, and as the drinks arrived, he turned to the waiter.

"His Eminence and I require a little privacy, if you could please." Victor motioned to the door and said, "*Prego*."

"Of course, your eminence. If you need anything, please just ring this bell." He handed Victor a large brass bell, old-fashioned but effective.

"*Grazie*." Victor smiled at the waiter, who had made the afternoon to this moment run very smoothly.

Martin's face dropped a little. "Down to business eh?" he said, tightening his jaw slightly. "I figured there was more than just missing an old friend."

Victor smiled warmly.

"But I did," he confessed. "I could have summoned you to the Vatican for this business. But I would like us to have this time as friends first. It has been too long."

"Yes." Martin loosened slightly.

Victor reached into his stylish black Prada leather slimline briefcase and extracted a yellow envelope.

"We have had some correspondence since your trip to Bangkok." Victor's eyes narrowed slightly as he placed the envelope on the table.

Martin was a little unsure whether he should open it. "Correspondence?" he said. "From the Cardinal. We made some excellent progress."

"No," Victor said bluntly. "Not from the Cardinal. I will start by saying the cardinal of Bangkok knows nothing of this."

Victor took a deep breath and let out a long sigh.

"From my understanding, nobody has any knowledge of this beyond the Secretary of the Vatican, the Papa, and myself." Victor paused and sighed. "Now you."

Martin's expression lightened. Was he being bought in on a top-level Vatican secret?

How exciting.

"May I?" he asked.

"Oh, and whoever took these photographs, of course," Victor added, motioning towards the envelope and giving Martin permission to inspect its contents.

Victor looked up again, drawn to the stunning surroundings. He had tried hard throughout the meal to focus on his friend, to read his face, hear his thoughts, and see if he could unearth the secret burned into Martin's soul.

But he could not.

He took a moment to absorb the beauty once more as Martin extracted the contents of the envelope.

Martin's face changed. A man who had recently been bought into the circle of trust at the highest level, was now pushed into the centre of that circle. He now lay waiting, ready to be whipped, beaten, thrashed and flogged until the blood that had drained from his face could erase the images in front of him.

"Victor," he said, defeated.

"Yes, Martin. Tell me, for the first time, a beginner's mistake." Victor had not scripted this moment and instead spoke from the heart. "How could you let the young one have a camera? A man in your position."

Martin's jaw tensed again. "No, not my first time with such beauty, Victor." Martin's face transformed into resignation. "But this is my first time falling in love. I just couldn't say no."

"Yes." Victor replied, willing himself to get away from that train of thought and into the realities of the offices they both held. Most importantly, the implications for the Pope and the Catholic Church.

"I am hoping whoever took these sent them to the Holy See, and we have contained the implications of these to a single person at the other end. At our end, we had three people; now we have four. We have paid a significant amount in response to the demand and received what we believe to be the original SD card. There is some video also."

Martin's head fell disconsolately. "In your hands, I can only beg for your absolution, your Eminence."

"Yes." Victor had a feeling that it would come eventually, but he needed a little more than that.

"Your penance shall come, my friend, and your absolution at the hands of the Papa. This is not my role. I am here for containment and to protect our holy church. Do you understand?"

"I do." Martin said, reaffirming his vows.

"I need the name of this young one, address, contact details, habits, hangouts, social media, everything you have; I need it without reservation. My requirement is to ensure that the containment at the point of origin is secure. We cannot run on faith in this matter."

"Understood." Martin had some details. In the last few minutes, he realised in his soul that love, sometimes categorised as intimacy, passion, and commitment, also needed to have an element of bilateral trust. Something he had shown but had not received in return.

"Treechada," he said, reaching for his digestive and sipping it thoughtfully.

"She is a teacher and was part of the focus group for the work the bishop and I were doing. The diocese's accommodation was fairly spartan in Bangkok, and the cardinal thought it would be better if I stayed in a hotel; he chose a very nice hotel. Five Stars." Martin was lost in the moment, and Victor listened patiently.

"I had not told anyone where I was staying, but on the second night, there she was, in the lobby. I was dressed in my street attire, and she asked if I would like a drink. So I did; no harm, right? The two of us talked for about two or three hours, a connection of minds and souls."

Martin's eyes closed, like he was savouring that memory.

"She took me on a fantastic tour of Bangkok at night, and as a good Christian, she dropped me off at my hotel. The next night, when I got back from my work at the Diocese, she was there again. This time, she took me to dinner, a traditional Thai meal, in an intimate, very private setting. I was lost, adrift in a world that I didn't know. I felt things I shouldn't have felt, and then she dropped me at my hotel again, but this time she accompanied me to my room."

Victor was now aware he had more work to do than first suspected. Hotel staff, restaurant staff, drivers and a whole range of possible ancillary people may be involved.

Martin continued. "When we got up to the room and it turned out she had additional equipment." Martin paused and swallowed guiltily "I hadn't realised before, they have amazing surgical techniques in the orient these days and with makeup and ..." Martin trailed off ashamed of his own shortcomings but knowing he needed to give Victor the whole story.

"Anyway, not my first tryst of this nature so I just ran with it. The week blossomed, possibly the most sublime week of my life."

"Since your ordination maybe." Victor added.

Martin looked back, a very guilty look.

The photographs were face down on the table. Victor picked up the bunch and looked through, looking for one in particular.

"... and this," he jeered at Martin.

The photograph was of Martin in a traditional Thai men's outfit praying at the large golden altar of a Buddhist temple. Martin's neck was barely holding onto his head, his self-esteem was a sunken treasure, lost to the light.

"Yes." Martin had nothing else to add.

"This is the worst of them all. How do we explain this?" Victor was leaning on his anger, trying hard not to show it to Martin.

Victor finished his digestive. "My car is arriving in ten minutes. Do you have anything else to add?"

Martin looked up with a torrent of abject misery erupting from the creases in his face.

"Victor. My friend. I am sorry I have caused you so much trouble."

"Yes." Victor hardened his resolve. "I have much to do."

He fixed Martin with his best authoritative stare.

"You will leave here now like things are great and we are just two friends having lunch. You will return home and pack for a prolonged stay in the Vatican. You will speak to no one. You will take the rooms next to mine, I have had them reserved. You will cancel plans to travel anywhere else and once you have received your absolution from the Papa you will cloister yourself in prayer and meditation until I come to pull you out of it."

"I will." Martin looked at Victor thankfully. This punishment was not so much a sanction as an isolation technique.

"You will not speak to another soul except the Papa and myself. You are officially taking a vow of silence to go with your extended prayer and meditation, so it's unlikely anyone in the Vatican will engage you in conversation, but in case they do, be prepared with a pen and paper. Tell them only that you are undertaking a vow of silence. If they ask why, say it's research."

"Understood." Martin managed a grimace. He was aiming for a smile but the muscles in his face just couldn't agree on position and tension.

It was probably better, Victor might not have appreciated a smile.

"I will be flying to Bangkok tonight but I have to return to London on Tuesday for a full Interfaith meeting on Wednesday. After that meeting, I will be following up in full."

Martin had nothing else to say.

Victor got up and, with his best theatre, thanked the house staff and the maitre'd, granting full compliments to the chef.

Leaving a crumpled Martin slumped at the table, he left for his waiting car.

Chapter Six

The Dalai Lama

United, we may stand

Jampa cloaked his life in service.

As private secretary for the Dalai Lama, Jampa got to meet interesting people, travel the world, and take on interesting tasks. Above all else, he had pledged his service to the greatest of all men, the Dalai Lama.

There was no doubt he had done something right in a previous life to reach such a position.

Jampa worked very hard to be the best he could be for His Holiness.

He had previously attended courses in time and international travel management, and he had most recently added Spanish to his fluent English, French, and Mandarin. COVID-19 had given Jampa time to brush up on things, but now that the restriction had been lifted, he was expecting that they would be back out on the road. Apart from his spiritual duties, the Dalai Lama was hot property on the speaking circuit. He had standing invitations from many famed universities and was regularly invited by governments and religious groups around the world.

The two of them travelled simply. They travelled in economy class where possible and liked to stay with local Tibetan families when they could, or if there was nothing suitable, they would stay in very modest accommodation, never elaborate or costly. The Dalai Lama didn't charge for any speaking duties. He was also not swayed by what people wanted him to say. He spoke from his heart with passion for the world, spreading the word of the Buddha using his own generous spirit and intellect to touch the souls of people of all faiths.

Jampa loved to quote his holiness. Words that seems to roll effortlessly from his very soul.

"Sometimes one creates a dynamic impression by saying something, and sometimes one creates as significant an impression by remaining silent."

This quote was his favourite, as he found himself keeping silent a lot unless he was required to speak.

"This will simply not do." His Holiness was reading the Times of India newspaper on his favourite chair. Jampa, as was his indulgence, kept silent. The truth would come out. He heard the newspaper page turn.

"It will not do." His Holiness was reading, thinking, and speaking.

It was rare, as the man had an ocean of patience. Jampa could hear him splutter.

"They cannot be serious, Jampa." His Holiness folded the newspaper and set it down, picking up his morning cup of tea to sip.

"Oh, that is still hot!" he exclaimed.

"Shall I cool it with ice, your Holiness?" Jampa offered.

"Time will cool it fine enough, Jampa. Thank you." Maybe his Holiness needed the ice, his face was reddening at the neck, like someone was slowly painting him crimson.

"This article states that on my passing the Chinese government will almost certainly move to pick a new Dalai Lama in Tibet, one who is expected to support the ruling Chinese Communist Party's control of the region. They simply cannot make that choice."

His Holiness shook his head. "I must respond."

Jampa knew better and kept silent. He was close by, supportive and listening, but silent.

"I need something with gravitas. My word alone seems to just ruffle the Chinese bureaucrat's feathers, leading to statements from them that were even more ridiculous than the first."

Early in his exile, the Chinese had him labelled a separatist, which is madness. He had agreed to Chinese rule if there could be some autonomy, preserving Tibetan culture and heritage. From his home in Dharamsala, India, his celebrity made him even more dangerous to the Chinese government. Even within China, Chinese people were sympathetic to his calls for genuine autonomy rather than independence.

"Perhaps now more than ever, the change in the mood of the Chinese people is a change in the mood of the Chinese government."

Jampa remained still and silent to allow His Holiness to voice his opinions unfettered.

"Maybe I could try to get the wider Buddhist community to show me some support. In the past, they have individually shown such support. If I could get the whole group together and get a statement that would have some weight."

"Don't you think, Jampa?"

Jampa had been asked many rhetorical questions by his holiness. Sometimes, like this, they came wrapped up looking like he was asking for Jampa's opinion, and while Jampa was not as wise as His Holiness, he had some wisdom of his own, at least enough to recognise rhetoric, especially when wrapped in a direct question.

"If your holiness thinks such a thing will help, then it must be the path."

His Holiness tilted his head slightly and stared past his cup of tea towards the wall in his office.

"I have so many supporters around the world, princesses, presidents, celebrities, and philanthropists, but my own community is often publicly silent in support of a free Tibet."

"I think we will need to go on the road again, Jampa."

"Yes your Holiness." Jampa had been expecting this.

"Let us organise a trip to Thailand, Myanmar, Japan, Vietnam, Sri Lanka, and South Korea."

"Yes your Holiness. I will contact the *Sangharaja*. Just a reminder, we have the interfaith meeting in London in three weeks where you are scheduled to address the whole religious community."

"Yes. I recall. It might be better, if possible, for me to have these meetings first to try to rally our Buddhist leadership. If we can act as a group and keep our differences out of the public eye, we may show unity never seen before."

"Yes, Your Holiness, a bold plan."

Buddhists have never been much for unity, but they are also not a divided group. As a religion based on tolerance, this includes tolerance of other beliefs and customs. So much so that in India, the birthplace of Buddhism, the religious following had pretty much died out until the Chinese invasion of Tibet in the 1950s, when Tibetans all crossed the border to get protection from India. At this stage, local Indian Buddhist practices had mostly been absorbed back into Hinduism, and mothers no longer passed on the traditions of the faith to their children. Buddhist monks tended to be cloistered and so not as active in the community as heralds of other religions, and as the message of the Buddha had been spread internationally, it was perhaps to the detriment of the message at its origins in India.

With the road beckoning, Jampa arranged everything for his Holiness. He booked flights, cars, and places to stay, and he did it fast. He saw his work as less of a chore and more of a pleasure, his role in the cosmos. Within a day, the two of them were flying to Thailand. The Dalia Lama began his tour in Thailand because he knew he would get a good reception. He was well known as the Thai *Sangharaja*, and he had many previous meetings and had so much common ground for agreement.

Jampa knew the two different teachings of the same faith had more similarities than differences.

Tibetan Buddhism focuses on the *Bodhisattva* ideal, a person who is on the path towards enlightenment. Whereas Theravada Buddhism, as predominantly practiced in Thailand, follows the *Arahant* ideal, where a being who has reached a state of perfection and enlightenment has achieved nirvana. Theravada is focused on the earliest record of the Buddha's teachings, usually known as the Pali

Canon. This Canon has then been interpreted through layers of commentaries and auxiliary works, and the sum of all these is what is now called Theravada.

Tibetan Buddhism, by contrast, is much more of a hybrid religion. Buddhism only fully penetrated Tibet from India at the beginning of the second millennium, and by this time, Indian Buddhism was quite different from what it had been at the time of the Buddha. Among other things, it was quite heavily influenced by Hinduism. In Tibetan Buddhism, you will see goddesses with multiple arms and Tantric practises, both imported from Hinduism. Tibetan Buddhism was also influenced by the local shamanistic religion known as Bon. Tibetan Buddhism emphasises visualisation as a method of meditation and mental development, whereas Theravada tends to focus on meditation such as mindfulness of breathing.

Jampa smiled to himself in his silence. He felt ready to offer assistance to His Holiness if needed.

The meeting in Bangkok went very well. The two men reached an agreement to work together, and the *Sangharaja* gave his tacit support for a Buddhist faith message on the cultural and religious autonomy of Tibet. Jampa was very happy for His Holiness.

The next stop was Vietnam.

It had been a while since Jampa had been to Hanoi, and the airport was unchanged and nothing less than atrocious. They had to wait such a long time for their bags and were just left standing in the cold arrivals hall. Very different from the treatment of holy men in Thailand, where special rooms or seating are set aside.

Hanoi had one 600-year-old Tibetan Buddhist pagoda, Long Quang. His Holiness had last visited to bless the restoration in 2011. The two were staying in the facilities attached to the pagoda, which was almost an hour's ride from the airport. The car driver was very friendly, as are most Vietnamese people. The Dalia Lama was a very open and warm person, and so the driver and his holiness maintained a conversation for much of the journey.

As they neared the pagoda, the driver asked the Dalai Lama for his advice.

He told a story about a lady from his village who was not having much luck. He said she tried everything to improve her fortune, including changing to just a vegan diet as per the Buddhist code, praying daily in her home, and attending the pagoda on temple days and holidays. With no change in her luck and at the behest of her neighbour, she took a trip to a local Christian church to pray. The next day, her luck changed. The thing she prayed for occurred. She was thankful, even if she felt a little uncomfortable. She then returned to the pagoda and, in time, found another sticking point where her luck simply would not change by following her old ways. She again went to the church and found that, immediately, her luck changed. She is now in a crisis and is attending church on Sundays and pagoda on holidays, and her family prayer area is now divided between the Buddha and Jesus Christ. What should she do now?

The Dalai Lama looked at the driver; his car was adorned with a Buddha, which was facing forward. The driver obviously cared for and prayed to protect himself and his passengers. He thought for a moment to collect his words. "The lady is looking to capitalise on opportunity, and it seems she found such opportunity in a church." His Holiness took another moment. "Without knowing the luck she desired or the Christian prayer that changed her life, I can only guess that it has come at the cost of some confusion."

The Dalai Lama coughed to clear his throat. "The poor lady now has two paths in front of her: one is her culture, her heritage, and her past. The other having the ability, it seems, to give her what she desires."

"She is not alone in facing this fork in the path. Many go down the road to desire and, in later life, try to rediscover the original path that family and community had put them on, to fill the void that desire creates."

His Holiness smiled and said, "I do know we must all follow our own paths as we see fit. The temples, churches, and holy men are just lights on the path sent to guide us, not to lock us in cages and force us. So we all must open our hearts and listen to find what path is best for us."

The driver nodded thoughtfully. "You are most wise, your holiness. I will convey this message. We are just two minutes from the pagoda. There will be someone to meet you at the door and take you inside. I will bring your bags in for you; please don't worry."

The two went inside and were shown some private rooms. The meeting with the Vietnamese *Sangharaja* wasn't until tomorrow morning, so they had some time. Jampa had several other things to organise, but first, using the house telephone, the two of them put in a call to the Taiwanese Buddhist Leader, hoping to get some time for His Holiness to discuss his plight and get Chinese

Buddhists to support or sympathise. It was also a good chance to discuss the upcoming interfaith meeting.

Going to Taiwan would create too much controversy, which the Dalai Lama was not trying to do. His last state visit to meet Barack Obama outraged the Chinese, so he thought better of such actions now. He hoped the Taiwanese would be understanding, as they had the potential to be in a similar plight as Tibet.

Jampa was very successful; he managed to get through to the leader of Fo Guang Shan (FGS), who has always had a great relationship with Buddhists in Beijing and the Chinese government in general. The current leader of FGS was relatively new in his position, with his predecessor having held the position for decades before passing only recently. The Dalai Lama and the new leader had met previously and were on good terms, if a little formal.

"Your Holiness, it is so good to speak with you." The FGS leader opened the call warmly.

"Most Venerable Bai Fang, thank you for your prompt attention." Jampa was staggered by how well his holiness handled himself in diplomatic situations.

"How is life in Dharamsala?"

"I am in Vietnam currently, trying to get some support for my Tibetan cause and consolidate the delegation for the Interfaith Conference in London. I would very much like to be having this conversation in person, but I thought it would just inflame tensions if I made a visit to Taipei."

The FGS leader choked slightly. "Yes, Your Holiness. As wonderful as it would be to host you here, a visit would be unwise, as you have said. What support are you looking for?"

The Dalai Lama outlined his need to respond to the Chinese with the support of Buddhists everywhere, protesting passionately that the government cannot simply choose the next Dalai Lama based on party lines. That such a thing is a holy act, performed by himself and his Tibetan community.

"Yes, I see your predicament. Can I be frank with you?" Bai Fang wanted to help but wasn't going to stick his neck out to have it chopped off.

"Please." His Holiness was open to support and guidance as always.

"I cannot possibly sign anything that would anger Beijing," Bai Fang began. "I caution you strongly not to release such a statement or create such a document. Such an action will not only not help your cause but will also bring other members of the faith into the firing line in Beijing. The Chinese Government needs little excuse to have further crackdowns on religious people bubbling discontent through what they call separatist talk." Bai Fang took a moment to consider his next words.

"With our help, we can mend the bridge that time has spanned between the Tibetan people and Beijing. You are doing a great job keeping your culture and heritage strong; if you can continue that work and we can broker some talks, you might find a better path. If you give Beijing a good reason, they might become your greatest ally rather than your enemy. This was the path of our great leader Hsing Yun."

The Dalai Lama hung his head slightly. Perhaps he knew these words to be true.

A leap of faith.

"You have strong friends who can help, but we are not strong enough to fight, just to smooth your path." Bai Fang's words were very wise.

The wise should always recognise wisdom.

"For the interfaith meeting," Bai Fang continued, "I will be in attendance personally, and I will bring others, people who have good links to China. We come representing two hundred and fifty million of the faithful. Let me get my assistant to discuss the details with yours. I will look forward to hearing you speak and being in your light again."

He didn't get what he wanted, but his Holiness was reminded that he must focus on the present and that what he had been given may just be what he needed.

The visit to Vietnam was a success, and like in Thailand, he received full support from the local Supreme Patriarch. The Vietnamese seem to have no fear of China, having repelled China before and France and America since they walked with an aura of invincibility woven through the fabric of their society.

His next visit was to Japan, where he met Kaito Kobayashi, the president of Soka Gakkai International. Kaito gave him similar advice to Bai Fang's caution when dealing with Beijing and a more moderate path.

Foster ties; don't burn bridges; keep your culture strong; but don't poke the Panda.

The Japanese contingent was confident things would change after the London meeting and was keen to attend. At least the Dalai Lama was having some success uniting the Buddhist collective.

Maybe that was his path.

He was his usual cheery, philosophical self, whatever the outcome. His next stop was Seoul and a meeting with Venerable Cheon, elected Supreme Patriarch of the Jogye Order. His order had been working hard to foster links with Chinese Buddhism but had had no luck with the government. The Venerable Cheon saw merit in the words of the Bai Fang and thought the continual antagonism of the Central Beijing government could only end badly for Tibet's faithful.

He got the same message in Sri Lanka.

Venerable. Anishka Chamara Tissera had recently been appointed chief of the Ramanna Nikaya Amarapura–Rāmañña Nikāya. He personally had no dealings with China but knew how hard it was to remain true to one's culture and heritage in this world. While he sympathised greatly, he said he would rather support the Tibetans changing to suit the times, as his group had done. On another positive note, he also confirmed he would be attending in London.

The final stop was Myanmar.

His expectations were low, as Myanmar had a difficult history and had recently locked up a number of monks, so the Dalai Lama had to tread lightly. He met the chairperson of the Sangha Maha Nayaka Committee. The meeting was very confusing. Jampa was a little unsure if it was a success or not.

"Greetings, Doctor Thandar. Thank you for seeing me." The Dalai Lama opened his body language and smiled to make the doctor feel comfortable. The doctor had a look on his face that could only be considered the polar opposite of comfortable; maybe it was the heat.

"Yes, Your Holiness, such a venerable man as yourself will always find an open ear in Myanmar," the doctor replied nervously.

"That is very gracious of you, Doctor." The Dalai Lama again tried to be warm, friendly, and open.

"I have travelled widely, visiting all our Buddhist brothers. I started in Thailand but also travelled to Vietnam, Japan, and Korea. I have also had contact with the FGS in Taiwan, trying to get support from our community for a united front to send a message to China to allow Tibet some autonomy to save our culture and heritage. I was wondering if you had some advice you could give or would support any communication I may have with Beijing to stop them from trying to appoint a puppet Dalai Lama."

A small bead of sweat rolled from the doctor's forehead, and he turned his head slightly left, like he wanted to ask a question, but there was nobody there.

The Dalai Lama was a patient man, and expecting an answer from the doctor, he waited.

For ten minutes, he waited before he elaborated. "Since the military invasion in 1956, my people have lived in India in exile, doing what we thought was right to preserve our Tibetan way. Can I ask if you will support the Tibetan people as part of a message to China from the Buddhist faith?"

The Dalai Lama felt that was very clear and waited again.

The Doctor again looked to his left; the Dalai Lama followed his gaze and found nobody there. The Dalai Lama again waited another ten minutes and received no reply. The sweat on the doctor's brow was now most pronounced.

"I understand, Doctor; thank you for your time." The Dalai Lama got up to leave, but finally, the doctor said something.

"I would dearly love to attend the Interfaith conference in London. But myself and my party are still waiting on confirmation of visas. Apparently, one of my party members was on some human rights list. We removed that individual, but still, the application is held up. Perhaps you could assist in getting these investigated."

The Dalai Lama was not just a patient man but a compassionate one as well.

"I will do my best, Doctor." He bowed lightly before turning to Jampa. "Is there an early flight we can get from here to get home, Jampa?"

"There is. I will make the change, Your Holiness." Jampa wanted to do his best, but in this case, he also felt very uncomfortable.

After two weeks on the road, the Dalai Lama had time for just two nights in his own bed before beginning his journey to London.

He had much to consider and much to do.

***

The Fleece for Cashmere and Pashmina

Jessica knew that with the Dalai Lama on board, the objective of the conference might just get over the line. Especially if he could use his celebrity to unite the Buddhists to agree on the unified faith concept. The two had previously had video link-ups for philosophical discussions on just this matter. How to collect together to be strong but preserve your own identity, culture, and history.

The Dalai Lama had shown himself to be a very knowledgeable man in all things. The discussions they had were not easy, and it was clear to Jessica early on that this would not be as easy as she imagined. Perhaps the slight pivot that the Anglicans made from the Catholic Church in the 1500s might align well with the differences between Theravada and Mayahana Buddhism, but between Christianity and Buddhism, there was a chasm that would be hard to bridge.

On the positive side, many Buddhists prayed to multiple gods and demi-gods, and the religion itself had tolerance for such things, if not in all things. Unlike her own version of monotheism, which preached tolerance in all things, except a lot of things.

The Dalai Lama was due to arrive in London on Tuesday. Jessica had offered to pick him up from Heathrow herself, but there was a large Tibetan community in London, and he needed to also be with them.

In some ways, Jessica was a little jealous of that. The Archbishop of Cantebury was meagre with his time in the community, preferring, as he put it, to have a hierarchical structure. Jessica chastised herself for her jealousy; it was not becoming. Somehow, she thought, the Dalai Lama must be the key.

Powering on in her Audi, on the edge of Oxford town, Jessica saw a small street store that sold woollen products. She had time, so she thought she would stop for a look.

She looked for a car park and, at first, wasn't able to find one. Bus zone, empty disabled parking space, empty parents with pram space, one small Nissan Micra in the oversized vehicles, nothing in the loading zone, and finally a Ford Raptor Ranger crammed into the small car parking space. Everything else was full, so she darted down a small side street, hoping to find a local who had gone out.

Indeed, the Lord shall provide, and she quickly grabbed the council-designated shoppers parking spot and walked back the six hundred metres to the shop. Jessica thought it looked like rain, so she made a note to be quick.

The store had the usual array of woollen products, tea cosys, knitwear, blankets, hats, and some pet products, but that was not what she was after. Tucked away in the corner was what she was looking for. Scarves.

She looked at what was on display. Pashmina, cashmere, and British wool scarves. The British wool scarves were beautiful, even though originally she had her mind set on a pashmina.

The sales lady noticed her indecision and saw an opportunity.

"Can I help you, Reverend?" she said.

"Bishop, actually." Jessica corrected her. "But Yes. I was hoping to get a scarf for a friend. Is the pashmina Tibetan pashmina by any chance?"

The assistant looked towards the door, like another customer might come in to save her. Seeing no one, she returned to Jessica. "No, I think you'll find pashmina is not from Tibet." The assistant gave the sentence a surety that Jessica was quite taken aback by.

"Well, what I meant was, are the goats from Tibet? Normally on the label, you have to say the country of origin, but this whole range seems to have the country of origin missing from the label.

"No, no, it's there." The assistant said, bustling past Jessica to show her. "There. There you go." She said, showing Jessica the label. "Oh, I see!" she exclaimed. "The labels are made in Tajikistan; it looks like they have printed the words "Country of Origin:" but missed out on what the actual country of origin is. Easy enough mistake."

"Are the scarves made in Tajikistan?" Jessica asked. Again, the assistant looked towards the door. "No," she said, like she spent most of her day explaining the obvious.

"The labels are not made where the scarf is?" Jessica queried.

"Crazy, isn't it?" the assistant agreed.

"I'm pretty sure this Pashmina is from Wales," the assistant said. "We try to keep all the products in here from the UK."

"So the wool is from a Welsh mountain goat?" Jessica asked.

"It must be." the assistant said.

"And the cashmere?" Jessica added

"Oh no, that's from Kashmir." the assistant clarified. "We can't call it cashmere if it's not from Kashmir."

"This label says Made in India." Jessica noted.

"Yes, it's a terrible shame, isn't it? Those labels are made in India, but the wool is from Kashmir. At least they got the label right in India."

Jessica said a silent prayer. "Right. I think I'll take the saffron British wool scarf. That is from the UK, isn't it?" she inquired.

"Yes, the wool is rever... erm... bishop," the assistant caught herself in time. "But it's assembled in Turkey, as part of one of those new EU deals. So we are allowed to sell them as British."

"Oh. That will have to be close enough then." Jessica had lost her will to shop, but soldiered on. "I was hoping to get it for a friend, something local, sort of a welcoming gift from the UK for someone arriving from abroad."

"That's nice," the shop assistant said. She was on board now.

"How about a tea cosy?" She pointed to the range near the counter, "made by the Men's Defence Against Domestic Violence Group. They are very soft and colourful, and they are great sellers."

"Yes, not really what I was hoping for." Jessica imagined explaining such things to the Dalai Lama.

She finished up the purchase and made a beeline for the door. It had started raining, not the usual British rain, more like a tropical downpour. With her purchase in hand, Jessica made a mad dash in the rain back to her car. Wet on the outside and thoroughly soaked on the inside, Jessica powered her car into action and blasted the heater.

As she did, the phone rang. The car screen showed David, Scientology UK.

"David." Jessica answered the phone brightly.

"Hi, Jessica. How are things? All geared up for the big show." David was the leader of Scientology in the UK.

"Great thanks." Jessica said, staying upbeat. "All good and ready to go."

"Splendid," David replied. "Do you have any room for more delegates?"

"Well, David, you must have read my mind." Jessica didn't want to sound flirty, but she was staying deliberately casual.

"I have someone, sorry, just one. But he wants a speaking gig." David changed his tone to be very formal.

"Yes. Speaking points to date are, the King opening on day one, the Dalai Lama opening on day two, then our Cambridge architect with our American marketing guru on day three, so we have a closing spot. What sort of address?"

David had been very patient but finally let the cat out of the bag. "Up front, Jessica, no beating around the bush. It's Tom. He wants to say a few words. I haven't vetted it; in my game, you don't vet Tom."

Jessica might have dribbled a little bit. "Tom!" she breathed out. "You're kidding me."

"Nope," David said. He wouldn't kid about that. "Tom heard your conference was happening and wants to give you all his support."

"Right. Done." Jessica wasn't turning down Tom. "Can he close? What a triumphant closing that would be."

"Yeah," David continued sounding somewhat evasive. Jessica prematurely pumped her fist in the air. "Tom is filming in Croatia all week, but he has Wednesday morning; he can only make it then. He will fly in and speak, then have to go. So maybe the opening. Can you bump the king?" Jessica's face turned to see the fog form on the outside of her car window.

"For Tom. Of course, Jessica was sure King Charles would understand and he would get the ending, which is almost the same.

"Great. His people have some security things they need confirmed, so I will put the main guy, Ari, in contact with you. OK. Tom needs a full house. You have a full house, right? The venue has eight hundred seats, and we only had one hundred and fifty at our last interfaith in Brussels, which was very disappointing." David sounded like he was closing off the call.

"Yes, of course." Jessica stretched the truth. "Brussels is pretty boring; who would want to go there? This is London. The venue will be full, standing room only, but I'll find a seat for Tom. Fantastic! You are truly wonderful. Thanks David. You made my week." Jessica's week hadn't been going that well, so the pivot was not hard to encourage.

"Great. Don't forget to save Shelley and myself a seat."

"Ha Ha. Of course David." Jessica smiled.

Shelley had been missing for 15 years.

David ended the call.

"Tom!!!" Jessica exploded, "Hey hey hey!!!"

Chapter Seven

It's Good to be The King

The Closer

Charles was a bit gutted.

"But it's Tom, Charles. You must understand they would be left with very little choice." Camilla was trying hard to console him. But when he gets into these moods, very little can bring Charles out.

"My dear, may I remind you that since Mummy left this mortal coil, I am the King?" He tried to hide it, but his best whiny voice was making his point clear: "Is Tom the King? Or is Charles the King?"

Camilla began to retort, but was beaten to it.

"Don't answer that." Charles got in first. "Is Tom the King of England? No. Are we in England? Yes."

"Yes, Charles, you are the King of England. But this is an international meeting of worldwide dignitaries from all of the great religious organisations on the planet." Camilla was trying to get Charles to see reason. She may as well have looked for the clown suit and the riding crop.

"Is the King of England still the head of the Anglican Church?" Charles knew the answer but was building his case. "Is To-om??" Charles made a screwed-up

ANDREW THURLOW

face, which was really not helping this conversation from degrading into a school playground screaming match.

"Charles!" Camilla berated, "Don't be juvenile. You are the King and the Head of the Anglican Church, but..."

Charles cut her off. "Don't say it."

"Don't say what." Camilla was not having much success.

"You were going to say, Tom."

Camilla bowed her head; she was indeed going to say Tom.

"You are just outgunned poppet; he is a global megastar, the biggest and brightest, and he's pretty much the face of Scientology. Apparently, they have more money than the Jews and the Catholics combined."

"Well, I am the king, so they can't have more money than me." Another juvenile countenance crossed Charles' weary, ageing face.

"It's the pen incident all over again." Camilla quipped, "The bishop of Oxford was ever so nice about the whole thing and has offered you the closing speech, which is a very important role as well."

"Oxford," Charles groaned, "if she were a he and he was from Cambridge, I would get the opening speech like Granddaddy always did."

"Now, Charles, we don't live in Granddaddy's world any more. The world has moved on. Every single dealing we have had with the Bishop of Oxford shows she is an extremely well-educated and capable person doing a fantastic job to keep the faith alive. Let's face it, the Archbishop is a bit of a flake, so someone needs to be the engine room of the Anglican Church or it will just fade away from pure lack of interest."

"What!" Charles spurted. "The Archbishop is a Cambridge man and a life-long friend."

"Yes, I know you are all Cambridge chummy, and he's a lovely chap, but sometimes he really needs someone to check he has his shoes on the correct feet. He may know a sermon or two, but his moments of clarity seemed to be only appearing at exponentially squaring intervals."

Charles had nothing positive to say about that, so he moved on.

"I thought we had gotten over the pen incident," he regressed.

"The pen incident is forgotten poppet. So let's get over this too. You have a chance to be the closer. Like Dave Chappelle. You do like Dave Chappelle, right?"

Charles did indeed like Dave Chappelle. There was a man who knew how to tell a story, almost as well as Ben Elton. Charles might have been a comedian if not for the whole King thing.

He smiled to himself, and Camilla smiled to herself. Job done.

"Is someone writing me a speech, or am I allowed to write my own? I do know a thing or two about religion, and I have read a synopsis of the girl's plan, which is beautifully architected."

"I believe the bishop has left it for you to write. She did ask if you could perhaps pop her a copy, just so she could read over it."

Charles had just taken a sip of tea and used all his significant years of society decorum not to spit the tea all over himself.

"The Oxford woman wants to check my work. Clearly, I am not the King."

"Well dear." Camilla needed to side with the bishop here, "you do have a history of going off track. They are aiming to have no sideline controversy over this. The bishop rightly thinks the content of the interfaith convention will be controversial enough."

"Going off track. *Moi.*" Charles said, rolling his lips over the French word perfectly. He liked French, but he liked German better. German was more real and meaty, while French was all flowers and aroma.

"Yes, dear. Should I list a few incidents?" Camilla knew them by heart.

"No." Charles put down his tea and stood ready to pace.

"Don't pace dear. You'll give me a migraine."

Charles sat again, got up again, and moved to the window. It was a dreary grey English day, much like yesterday, and except for the short period between eleven and eleven forty-five tomorrow, according to the Teletext weather, much like tomorrow would be. Charles also liked Teletext; like German, it was real; no poncy weatherman or under-dressed weather girl to muck it up. It just was. Mostly, it was wrong, but at least it was real in its wrongness.

"The Closer," Charles said out loud.

He walked to the servant rope and pulled it once.

An immaculately dressed young man entered the king's private rooms and stood quietly.

"Yes, Peterson." Charles said. He was on a surname basis with everyone at his private house in Llwynywermod. "Get a hold of Forester to pass a message to Blinken that I am good to be "The Closer" on the final day of the Bishop's show in London."

"The closer, your Majesty. Absolutely."

The house staff were under instruction to reply back to Charles in a shortened form of the task he had asked them to perform. Hopefully, it would prevent a repeat of the hose pipe incident. This boy she could kiss, his choice of words couldn't have been more perfect.

"Yes." Charles smiled a Cheshire Cat smile. "The Closer"

Camilla left it at that.

She didn't have the heart to remind Charles he was actually opening the last day.

***

The Opener

Tom was not nervous.

Very few things made him nervous these days because Tom is, well, Tom. He knew that whatever life threw at him, he had this.

Tom had spent thirty years with an unbreakable belief in Scientology. It had made his resolve immovable, his bravado unshakeable, and his confidence unstoppable.

You get the picture.

Of course, some of those things might also have to do with his bank balance, which, despite some extraordinary spending habits, was still astronomical. That sort of money breeds that sort of confidence. The sort of confidence that would lead an actor in an elite class all of his own to want to stand up and tell a bunch of highly educated religious people how he felt about Scientology.

That was Tom, ready to spread the word. He wasn't here to listen; he was here to talk.

His latest movie was filming in Croatia, and he was on a seriously limited time frame. So he needed to get in, speak, and get out. He would pay for it all, the helicopters, private jets, and security. Actually, he was going to be fronting security for the whole show.

Before Ari got involved, security was just one old guy. He might have been called the doorman, but it was an automatic door. He wasn't checking tickets, IDs, or even stopping anyone from coming in. He was just wearing a badge that said security.

When Ari saw that. Well, if Ari had had hair, he would have lost it all in a pile on the floor.

So Ari fixed it so Tom would be safe, and as a side gesture, Tom let the security detail stay for the whole three days.

The truth is, Tom was paying for four days, as that was the working minimum. Tom really only wanted one day, but that's just not how things work in the UK. Ari said to Tom that they were the best security detachment in the UK and could only be secured in lots one week at a time. The week was further narrowed down to a working week, but they were trying out a four-day working week and loving it so far. It meant they would work between eight a.m. and five p.m. four days a week instead of five. If you needed longer coverage, they could get the second crew to come in and cover, and if full 24-hour coverage was needed, there was an A, B, and C crew that you could mix and match depending on the skills you wanted. That was great, but Tom just needed one hour in the morning on Wednesday. Possibly an escort from London City Airport and some ground support. Ari thought it was important that the grounds were swept before Tom arrived, and while enquiring, Ari found out what the security was like and took over.

Eight hundred of the world's top religious scholars and no security wouldn't cut it for Ari.

The bishop seemed very happy to hand security over to Ari; it wasn't that she didn't understand security or care; she just had a million other things she needed to deal with. The bishop had confirmed that Tom could write his own speech. He thought carefully about what would be a good subject and could see only one.

Tom's journey with Scientology.

Tom didn't have a device to write a speech on. He was beyond devices; he had people for that. But he wanted this one to come from the heart, so he commandeered a pen from one of the makeup girls and used the back of the title page of the script of the movie he was working on. He thought a page would do.

Tom had all the scripts he worked on printed.

If there was a change to a part involving him, he had a lady come and give him a whole new script. For a while, she would just replace pages that had changed, to save paper, but then she got one wrong, and Tom had two pages the same but different and another page missing. So he replaced her instead and got someone who did it the way Tom liked it done. To make himself feel better, Tom donated some tax-deductible money to get some trees planted.

It was sizeable money because he was Tom.

Tom started his speech. As he did when he read movie scripts, Tom projected himself forward into the moment.

"When I was younger, I was ambitious. I wanted to be the best actor on the planet. Once I had that and all the trimmings that came with it, I found myself lacking something in my life. I got married, and my then-wife showed me what Scientology was all about. I liked it, but a few years later I found the wife not really fitting. So I met another wife and found some kids, but still, something was lacking. Some of the movies I have made are really good; some are just me making them good; and in others, I surround myself with the best people. So I think the ones that aren't so good are from a time before I really understood

Scientology. So today I would like you to see the three tenets through the eyes of Tom.

Tenet Three: Human beings possess infinite capabilities. I really believe that, and I put my trust in people who also believe that. I shoot my movies by placing trust in people, but I push them hard to be just as good as I am. You just can't mosey through life when you are with Tom."

Tom smiled that multi-million-dollar smile. His face was aligned symmetrically to accentuate all the best facets of all men and somehow reflect the light perfectly from every angle.

"So, tenet two says that we will transcend a single lifetime, and I know a few of you out there aren't disagreeing with us there."

Tom took a pose and pointed both forefingers and thumbs, pistol style, at the imaginary Dalai Lama and the Buddhist contingent who were sitting listening to him.

"The final tenet is that we are immortal. Now you really have to unpack the word immortal and what that means. It's not like a Marvel Immortals kind of thing, because that stinks a lot. It's more that we live forever, if not in this body and this face." Tom curled his hands around his body and his face; he felt it was easier for people to visualise if he accentuated it. "In another body with another face, we are learning lessons and doing our thing until we get it. The best I can say is that it's helped me a lot on my personal journey, and I think you all should look into it and see that perhaps it's not so bad."

"Perfect," Tom said aloud.

***

The Guru

Marcus was regretting not getting someone else to do all the presentation slides.

He had intended to spend the second leg of his flight from Richmond, Virginia to London, working on the presentation. The flight from Richmond to Washington was only an hour, and he had taken the time to relax by watching a streaming TV episode he had previously downloaded on his laptop. When he got to Washington, he found that his flight had been considerably delayed, so he enjoyed another episode in the lounge over a snack and a few glasses of his favourite Kentucky Bourbon.

When Marcus' flight finally was due to leave, he found that while he had plugged into the power point in the lounge successfully, the power points were locked out and he hadn't noticed. His battery was down to just 15%. To make matters worse, once he boarded the flight, the replacement plane was not the super-new 787 Dreamliner as he had been expecting but a 1980s 767-300, which had no power points fitted, even in business class.

So with a 15% battery, he had cobbled together what he could, thinking he could polish the rest in the morning in the car. After the flight, in his hotel, he had forgotten to reset his alarm after his morning flight and woke up at some ungodly hour. He then switched off his phone completely instead of the alarm and overslept considerably. Lucky for Marcus, he remembered to charge his laptop overnight and so got most of the work done on the car ride from the Heathrow Hilton to the convention center.

London traffic didn't appear as bad as everyone had said. No worse than most of the cities in the US. He did wonder why they had reduced what was effectively a lane and a half in most places to a single lane to allow for a bicycle lane. It rained all the way in, and Marcus counted just three brave cyclists in his one-hour and fifteen-minute drive among the thousands of cars on the M4 and A4.

Marcus had missed Day One. It appeared that Tom was the opener. Holy damn, if Marcus had known that, he would have gotten in earlier. All the documentation said it was going to be King Charles, so Marcus decided to stay in Richmond and get some work done.

Thanks to his missed alarm, he had also missed breakfast, and he had also missed the Dalai Lama. When he arrived, he found security had marked him as absent, so he wasn't allowed to enter the lunch hall. He was pretty hungry, so he quickly got a bite to eat at the Pret-a-Porter next door.

Marcus' life just seemed littered with bad decisions. He was only allowed into the main auditorium after a call to the Bishop of Oxford, who escorted him past the thugs masquerading as security. He was seated at the back for Maryam's presentation and attempted to take as many notes as he could.

She was bold, intelligent, and organised.

Fantastic.

He was looking forward to working through this with her. If he could, he would grab her before the day was done and try to get some one-on-one time.

When the squabble broke out, Marcus didn't see who started it.

It was all a bit of a blur as he was trying to take notes, but some guy just came out of nowhere and looked like he was going to try and take the stage. If anyone had asked him later, he wouldn't have been able to describe what the guy looked like; he was just like any other guy. Regular height, regular build, regular clothes. Oh, wait, Marcus thought he had a beard, and was that long hair or just a big beard? Anyway, it was over in a flash; that security team treated him very roughly.

Marcus wasn't able to get a hold of Maryam after the show had finished.

She seemed to be needed in every power huddle led by the bishop. Marcus didn't really know who the people were, so he didn't feel he should interrupt. Instead, he found a Hindu, a Buddhist, and a Catholic from Singapore talking in a group. Marcus was a pretty open guy, so he chatted with them. He found out in a very short time that Singapore has a very tolerant mix of the three religions, and even some Jews, Sikhs, and Taoists are in the mix.

He tried to equate that to Richmond, where it was overwhelmingly Christian.

The truth is that the next most dominant religious group after Christianity was "No Religion."

He was pretty sure there were some Jews and Muslims around, but they kept pretty quiet as the aforementioned Christians weren't so tolerant. The Muslims in Richmond were not like the Muslims here at the conference; they were brotherhood. It looked to him like none made the cut here, but they were noisy in Richmond.

Marcus moved on to another group, who were Kurds. Marcus had never met any Kurds that he knew of. Wow, he learned a lot from them about persecution, genocide, rebellion, and the pursuit of autonomy, independence, and cultural rights. Serious guys, those ones.

He pondered, thinking this was supposed to be a religious gig.

After a quick word with some Presbyterians, he managed to strike up a conversation with some Japanese Shintos.

Who would think religious people were such fun?

The whole Shinto group invited Marcus to a Japanese restaurant for dinner, and they all hit the Saki hard. Marcus had a great time and felt like he had really picked up on the vibe of the conference. He got a call about 7 p.m. from the Bishop of Oxford and had it confirmed that tomorrow he would be on after the king gave the conference closing speech to work through the implementation of Maryam's plan before the actual close of the conference.

It looked like Marcus had messed up somewhere; he was sitting through the king's speech after all. Marcus made a note that he would have extra-strong coffee in the morning. Maybe one of those small, dynamite espresso coffees the Italians always went on about.

Drunk as a skunk Marcus fell into bed around one a.m.

Chapter Eight

Between Death and Resurrection

London Calling is by The Clash

The second day of the conference opened with little fanfare. Like many second days on the conference circuit, this is a meat and potatoes day, hopefully not pork, and at this conference, definitely Halal. The introductions are over, old acquaintances are reunited, hands are shaken, new friends are made, and so we get down to business. There was an early breakfast for the delegates in the dining room that cascaded off the main auditorium, and so by the time everyone was in their seats and settled, it was closer to ten thirty than ten.

The room lit up as the Dalai Lama took to the rostrum. For those who were listening to His Holiness for the first time, the anticipation was palpable. For others, they knew what to expect and knew the following hour would not be wasted. His focus today was on togetherness and the unity of faith in a world that seemed unclear about the role faith would play in the future.

"Whatever it may be," he quipped, "I shall be there."

His speech was followed by lunch.

The main business of the day was for Maryam to give her presentation. Maryam was perfectly prepared with a shortened version of the overall plan in dot points to make it easy. Similar to what she showed the Hindu Council.

Maryam introduced herself as a Hindu, originally from India but now study-ing and residing in Cambridge in the final year of her PhD studies. She went through her first scholarship, her second, and the reason she was here, her scholarship to Cambridge. She then gave thanks to her parents and Vishnu before starting.

Her outline of a world in decline needed no support. She had some graphs on resource scarcity, lopsided values, wealth inequality, and a lot of blame on climate change, which had questionable science cherry-picked from a mass of data to back it up. She touched briefly on the representations of greens in government in the climate change debate and the definite twisting of what the solution should be.

A decisive crack between so-called experts, government, and reality.

Maryam continued highlighting that most of the green solutions came in the form of products that were 'green' alternatives to existing products without clear research on how that change of product would affect climate change. One such product that Maryam highlighted was the all-conquering EV. The EV uses less fossil fuels, not "no" fossil fuels as some marketing may suggest, as there are fossil fuels used in plastics, rubber, steel, etc. EVs future also begged the question of the long-term waste storage of battery cells and the devastating production of Lithium on the water and soil. There was also, of course, the fact that electric cars still use the biggest cause of climate change (undisputed), which is tarred roads. In many jurisdictions, the fact that electric cars did not pay any road levies meant many roads would fall into disrepair as the money dried up from fuel excise, releasing toxins into waterways. The world also had a mixed network of renewable and fossil fuel power. Most consumers could not tell the difference. But EVs just plugged in and charged without caring about the power source, leaving many of them operating on so-called fossil fuel power, which was in itself the very thing EVs and other such products were trying to get rid of. Even though in many cases this is better than petrol, more research was needed to get the full impact.

Maryam moved on to the growth of the green movement, whose history every-body knew. First, just a bunch of hippies saying things need to change, some protests, some changes. But then, in the 1990s, perhaps thanks to Steve Jobs, the green movement saw a new vanguard in the form of yuppies and new tech wealth. They used that to front political candidates and run for office based on a platform of radical but local change. Now, thanks to significant government pressure and Arnold Schwarzenegger, these green advocates have enticed mums and dads and grass-roots organisations. pushing a shift in policy due to incontrovertible data that was too complicated for average people and was interpreted by people you just needed to trust. Using these tactics, they have captured a significant part of the faith market. While traditional faith in traditional gods declined.

Several non-affiliated wall-dwelling insectoids in the room smiled silently to themselves, thinking of a pot and kettle coexisting, perhaps showing the true colour of God.

Maryam continued, outlining that in all free elections around the world, people no longer go to an election looking for the opinion of the local priest, monk, imam, or swami. They don't get the information from us that one candidate has performed excellent community service and has strong moral values. They are left with a choice: believe the traditional "in it for themselves" candidate or go with the simpler option and vote Green. The majority of people now see the Greens as a safer faith alternative.

Maryam bowed her head slightly to continue, "The image today left by many religions is, unfortunately, the headlines." She paused and put a slide of newspaper headlines on the screen. "Girlfriend claims monk is three times married with children. Swami makes questionable advances to entourage members of meditating celebrities. Sexual mistreatment of minors by priest."

"This is baggage each faith carries. All of this has been something the Green Movement, in its infancy, has not had to deal with. But it will. How do we fight back? I present to you a possibility." She paused for a moment to allow the full extent of her opening to sink in.

"My thesis contains a lot of mathematical probability, in the first few pages is the probability of the monotheist religions consolidating. The probability is very high and we already see consolidation in folk and fringe religions. It is possible we can just let it happen, or we can help it along in an orderly way. That is up to this group that gathers now and those that will come after us." Maryam had paused again to take a drink of water.

"I am here today presenting you my life's work as I believe you are the only group who can actively work with governments globally to enact this change. You carry with you the faith of the world on your shoulders. These changes can make a difference to our planet and turn the world's gaze back from the sham science that is green politics to the true faith."

Maryam receives thunderous applause as the lights go up.

ANDREW THURLOW

The loudspeaker announces a break for coffee and tea.

***

The Semi Caffeinated Cardinal

Victor was very impressed. The girl had charisma, intelligence, and passion. He had not known many Hindu women, but if this is the strength they convey, no wonder they got along so well.

First things first, Victor thought.

Coffee.

If there is one thing Victor knew about London, it is that the coffee was horrendous. For some reason, the English could make tea of the finest quality. Prepare it. Filter it. Pour it and leave it for just the right amount of time in that process to make drinking it a wonderful experience.

If you liked tea.

Why then, thought Victor, is coffee such a confusing chore for them? He had personally petitioned the CEO of Illy to open coffee shops in London and train these wayward people to follow the basic steps of coffee preparation.

So today, even though he had asked the Bishop of Oxford for espresso on the menu, what did he see?

Yes.

Cappuccino.

"I should be able to get this," he thought to himself.

Victor presented himself to the coffee line and waited a few minutes behind a few other people. He was happy to wait and consolidate his thoughts around what the girl had said. He took it all in, especially the part about the minors, horrible business. He watched the small woman making the coffee, her hair shaved on one side, the trailing ends of tattoos reaching for air from the arms and neck of her black button-up shirt. She had obviously removed some metal from her face for this work. 'Can she make coffee though?' he pondered. The other things were OK if she could.

Victor reached the front of the line and received greetings from a very fat, very flustered-looking white pasty man. The shirt of the barista was perfectly proportioned, but clearly, the sizes only went up to XL, and this particular guy was well beyond that.

"Right Luv," he began his spiel. "Today we have cappuccino, latte, or hot chocolate. What would you like?"

"I would like espresso, please. Cappuccino without milk in a small cup." Victor was very clear.

"Oh, sorry, Luv, but that's not one of the options. If we make an exception for you and all the others, we'll be here past dinner time. One from the list and your name, please."

Victor shuddered slightly. "*Café nera, prego.*"

"No problems, lovely." The large man wrote something on the cup. He was sweating profusely, but Victor wouldn't have thought it was that hot in the room.

"Next!"

A rather large Syrian imam was behind Victor and pushed past him to get his order in.

Victor was not impressed. He was considering his options when he was intercepted by the Bishop of Oxford with Maryam in tow.

"Cardinal. It's nice to finally meet you in person. I am Jessica, the Bishop of Oxford. Can I interrupt and introduce Maryam to you? Maryam, this is Cardinal Marietti from the Vatican."

Up close, Victor noticed that Maryam had a very kind face; she presented him with such a beatific smile. "Pleased to meet you, your eminence," she said.

"Yes, I am pleased to meet you also, Maryam. What a rousing opening address."

"Thank you, your Eminence. A passionate subject close to my heart."

"Preggo. Cappuccino for Preggo" The barista's voice projected like an air raid siren across the crowded room.

"I am looking forward to the reaction of our faith family here to what you have to say. I think we in the Catholic Church can see the benefits of your wisdom; we just need to gain consensus."

"That's very encouraging news, Your Eminence." Jessica added.

"Preggo. Second Call. Cappuccino for Preggo and a Latte for Bassam." The large Syrian imam moved forward to collect his coffee.

"How is our mutual friend Martin?" Jessica enquired.

Victor visibly blushed. "He is taking some time out. I had forgotten you two were friends." Victor added.

"Yes," she said. "He was in Bangkok the last time I heard from him. Having a wow of a time."

"Preggo last call. Hot chocolate for Elton!" the barista cried in a sing song voice giving a contertenor performance for the name Elton.

Victor realised the mistake and moved slightly to his left towards the counter.

"I am Preggo for the cappuccino." He figured if he couldn't get espresso, he would take what he could get, securing the coffee and returning to face Jessica and Maryam.

"Preggo your eminence?" Jessica queried.

"Not really. Just enjoy *Nona's* pasta," he smiled. "It's so hard to get good coffee in your country, bishop."

Maryam stood quietly and smiled. "We know some great places around Oxford and Cambridge, your Eminence, but unfortunately, London can be a bit of a wasteland. If you are ever in Cambridge, please let me know and I will make sure you get a *bellissimo espresso*."

"Indeed. *Grazie*, my child." For the moment, Victor would just have to make do with what he had.

***

I really need to know

Hasan needed to interject. One of the *Bani Shaiba* was trying to find out if the pastries were Halal. Unfortunately, his English was very rusty.

"*Iz mueajinat... halal.*" He was trying to form the words with his hands as he spoke, hypnotising the attendant momentarily.

Hasan interrupted and let the key bearer know he had been assured the pastries were halal. In response the concerned key-bearer pointed out to Hasan the knob of butter hanging from the end and the names on the trays.

"Right." Hasan said, touching his head and bowing to his very important brother. "I will check for you."

He turned to the attendant.

"Hi." He said loudly. "Are you sure these pastries are Halal?"

"The sign says they are." The attendent said, looking a little peeved.

"Yes, the sign does say that. Can you tell me if they were made on-site or delivered in."

"The kitchen here is very pokey." The attendant flicked his red hair to the left and said, "had to be delivered; they came in this morning."

"Great," Hasan replied, "and all the pastries are from Rinkoff Bakery, or just the Halal ones."

"Rinkoffs were pretty pricey, so we just got the Halal ones from them. The rest are from the Chinatown Bakery."

"Perfect." said Hasan, trying to be positive.

"Did you stack the display yourself?" He was clearly not giving up.

The attendant started to look shaky and defensive.

"They are just sweet pastries. Nothing in the cabinet is pork or beef."

"Wonderful!" Hasan smiled. "Did you pack the cabinet?"

"I was here," the attendant said, now being very non-committal. "The Rinkoffs went in the far end where the sign for Halal was, and the others went in next to them."

As the attendant finished speaking, a small African guy came in and removed an empty tray of pastries, then replaced it with another. Hasan looked closely, as they appeared to be the same as the ones where the Halal sign was and had a Rinkoff Bakery paper underneath.

"I think you might have mixed things up." Hasan said nicely. "This man behind me is the keeper of the keys to Mecca. He has lived 100% Halal his entire life."

The attendant appeared to be very uninterested.

"If he breaks his pledge, he would need to relinquish his most important post, and this will bring shame on his family."

"It's just a pastry." the attendee said, very sure it was just a pastry.

Hasan turned and smiled at the Bani Shaiba brother. "Your wife called, my brother. She said, You must cut down on these while you are away."

He rubbed his own belly.

"Not Halal," the Bani Shaiba brother said in his perfect Arabic.

"I'm not 100% sure," Hasan replied. "Better not to risk it. We are having dinner in a fantastic Turkish restaurant later; you should save your appetite."

The Bani Shaibi looked crestfallen but remembered his manners. "Thank you, Imam, for caring for my soul."

"1-nil, 1-nil, 1-nil."

Hasan turned to see Yitzakh behind him doing a dance. Yitzakh pulled aside his robe to show a Tottenham Hotspur jersey underneath.

"My friend, you will roast in Hell with that thing on," he smiled, and the two warmly embraced.

"Ready for the big announcements?" Yitzakh asked.

Sadly, many of my brethren are just here for the cakes, and now I find out they might not be Halal."

Yitzakh's face fell. "So not Kosher either." Yitzakh signalled to the man he was with to stop eating.

"What's the problem?" Ari shouted.

"Not kosher." Yitzakh replied.

"But I have had three already." Ari confessed.

Yitzakh introduced the two men. "Hasan, this is Ari. An old Krav Maga sparring partner."

"Greetings Ari." Hasan had seen the large man on the first day. He wasn't wearing any security markings like the others.

There seemed to be a few of them fawning over Tom.

"Ari is on security. Usually as Tom's personal guy, but Tom loaned him to us."

"Hasan is the Imam for North London's biggest Islamic Community Centre."

"Do I eat this?" Ari asked Yitzakh.

"How is your soul, brother?" Yitzakh asked with a serious face.

Ari took another bite.

"Compromised by way more than a Danish."

Yitzakh frowned.

"We are strange bedfellows, aren't we?" Jessica had been watching from across the room and came into the conversation with Maryam in tow.

"Old friends and new." Hasan replied.

"Yitzakh is the President of the Jewish Council in Israel. Ari is his friend, and..."

"Yes, Ari and I have met." Jessica was surprised. "How do you two know each other?" she asked, pointing to Yitzakh and Hasan.

"School friends from Cambridge," they replied in unison.

"Great." Jessica said with an air of resignation. "Well, I'm outgunned here. Gentlemen, this is Maryam, also a Cantabrigian."

The three shook hands as the lights flickered to return to the auditorium.

"Cakes OK?" Jessica asked as Ari filled his mouth with the remainder of the Danish.

"Apparently a mix-up with what's Kosher and Halal and not." Hasan chimed in.

"All ordered and delivered, but the display was not clear, so I steered the Muslims away."

"Ari here got in too early, but we will leave it also," Yitzakh added.

"Really," Jessica exclaimed, "do these catering people not know the rules?"

The four moved in towards the auditorium as one.

Full of Danish, Ari surveyed the room menacingly.

***

Keeping it all on Track

Maryam was not nervous; her confidence was brimming.

Much of the presentation was for her to run through and explain. If people were not happy, they could comment, but this was more informational than anything. A detailed debate will follow tomorrow after everyone had time to digest the grand scheme.

She started her first slide confidently.

The first slide was Education.

Surprisingly, nobody had any comments, and there were even several nods of approval. She talked over the points methodically and added just enough emotional impact to let the conference know this was important. They all knew education was the shield against ignorance and tyranny. She moved on to her next slide, noticing the huge smile of pride on the Lutheran representative from Finland.

The second slide was Existing Population.

Nobody doubted Maryam's figures, and while there is some trepidation about what these population figures mean, Maryam quickly dispelled that by outlining that according to the World Health Organisation, there is enough to go around. Plenty of land, and plenty of resources if we share and allocate things properly. The Greens may sing doom to get support from disaster, but based on technical data from the WHO, the UN, and others, the planet can handle it if we all use resources wisely. Historically, there have been weather accounts that explain what is happening as the earth shifts and moves.

Not every storm has a human cause.

Some experiences we are having now are just repeat incidences of similar documented weather events thousands of years ago. If the Greens looked beyond the last hundred years of meteorological data to what we have in the texts of the faiths, they would see that. But to a troubled infant, everything is doom and gloom.

She moved on to the third slide.

The third slide was Infrastructure.

Maryam moved through the content, putting on display her knowledge of her subject and her empathy for the people it affected. She was interrupted during section three, part three, on recycling and the sharing of technology by one of the Cambodian Buddhist representatives, who, during a quiet moment, asked in a very quiet voice. "How are we supposed to get governments to do things? Some of these matters are surely not for religious groups but for the government."

Maryam looks towards Jessica as to how she should answer. Never one to leave things unsaid, the Mahant chimed in, "We must adapt and lobby the government for change for the better." His strong, authoritarian voice left no doubt.

"If we can find consensus, I can help lobby Israel's *Knesset* to share our technology. I have seen it in action, and it is amazing." Yitzakh's powerful, warm voice filled the room.

Maryam added "If we work together, things will happen that will show positive change. That is how the green movement is trying to garner support through political lobbying and representation. They are doing it across countries' borders, but we have better communications and better community networks than they do. In answer to your question, you may lobby yourselves, but it would be better if you looked to your faithful to help you."

Maryam continued, "We must tell people about this too, making sure our success is highlighted rather than our indiscretions."

The Baptist representative piped up.

"Lobbying the government is a very murky business. The last time a Baptist lobbied the government for change was when Dr. King got shot." He left that hang to let the room know this was not beer and skittles.

Maryam was sure in her reply: "There are subtle ways to lobby as a faith group working together. As the very wise Rabbi alluded to, such lobbying should try to be less confrontational and more cooperative, unlike the Venerable Dr. King, who really had to go out on a limb to enact real change."

There was a respectful hush around the room; everyone knew the sad end to the story of Dr. Martin Luther King Jr.

"With all due respect, my dear," the Baptist minister broke the silence. "Kind as your words may be to the late Dr. King, what could a young Indian girl possibly know about him? India had never had to fight for anything. India had everything handed to them by the British. Americans had to fight tooth and nail, and Dr. King gave his life to ensure the equality we enjoy in the USA today."

Jessica gave Maryam a windup sign, and she quickly changed slides.

The fourth slide was Population Control.

When the slide for Section four, Part two, 'Better redefine incentivised wealth equalisation' is shown. Victor, who had just taken a sip of water from his conference-provided recyclable plastic bottle, spat it out exclaiming, "Wealth Equalisation! Are we giving all our money away now?"

THE COLOUR OF GOD

Maryam looked at Victor calmly. "No, your eminence." she began. "However, there is a need for a modification of economic behaviour for all faiths. While this meeting is convened in part to deal with the green faith issue, there are also deeper problems we have to address. We must set examples for the faithful; if we share interfaith, then they will be more open to listening to our words. We must look at the reasons why movements like the Islamic Revolution, Dr. Martin Luther King's Civil Rights Movement, and India's own venerable Mahatma Gandhi's push for independence gained such wide religious support but not support from the government of the day." Maryam allowed herself a sneaky look at the Baptist minister, who seemed to be listening intently but didn't register the comparison.

"These often violent uprisings are usually precipitated by the inequities of life becoming too much for a certain group. There is a need to push a message that will inevitably mean those with, will either lose everything as in the case of French King Louis XVI or in the case of the British in the US and India." She again passed a quick glance at the Baptist delegation and then realising she had done this again said a little prayer to Ganga the god of forgiveness.

Maryam returned her focus to the moment, presenting herself resolutely.

"This report takes the best out of many systems and looks at the failures of structures in capitalism, autocracy, theocracy, communism, and others, addressing possible modifications to ensure those failures are better dealt with within our faith structures. Above all, we should do as we say. Show the world if we can work together, that they can too."

Maryam was confident in her words and continued, "So my suggestion, if you don't want to lose everything, is that you consider certain changes to your existing way of operating."

Victor's face changed slightly, and he placed his hands gently back in his lap.

"Well, that's just not what is expected in the Catholic Church. People believe we are strength, we are eternal, and we are the voice of God."

There was a general silent agreement in the room that indeed, that is what people believe, mostly from the representatives of the big four religions. In stark contrast, there was fierce debate from a lot of other representatives. The representatives from that group barely spoke for five percent of the people on the planet; however, from the noise in the room, it could be said the people wanted change.

Maryam quickly changed tack. "Everyone's opinion deserves to be heard. The opinion of the Catholic Church as the largest of all our groups is very important to the future of all religious movements."

Victor allowed himself a small smile. Jessica also smiled and thought 'Good girl'.

Maryam continued, "As calm, educated members of such a wide range of religious organisations, perhaps it is wise if we hold any further questions to the conclusion of the presentation when we can look at this cut-down part of the plan in the context of the whole."

She displayed the next slide, "Population Control," and the possible introduction of a birth licence.

Victor let out a loud groan and stood up, ready to walk out, waving his arms in a very Italian way. Many of the other Catholics were surprised and prepared to join him, but Jessica was waiting nearby. Jessica stopped Victor and gestured for all the representatives to please stay in their seats.

She took Victor by the elbow and whispered quietly, "Martin sent me a few photographs of his Bangkok trip." She looked him in the eye. "If you stay here and help, the outcome might just draw the news hounds away from his pictures, if they ever get out, and instead focus those lenses on the good we do at these interfaith things, in the face of often extenuating circumstances."

Victor raised his eyebrows and duly returned to his seat. He signalled to the rest of the Catholics that they would stay. Not to be outdone, he shook his head and said loudly "I just can't see how I will get the college of cardinals to even consider such a thing."

Maryam, feeling the tension, moved on to the final slide.

"Cardinal, I think we all know the history the Catholic Church has with this issue. You are alone in your faith on this, but it needs to be taken into account if we are to succeed. Let's leave this issue for the future, shall we? Tomorrow is to allow us to better look at these issues and how we can compromise and find common ground."

The fifth slide was Social Changes.

During the scuffle over population control, while Jessica was keeping the Catholics in the room, several other groups left behind her back.

There might have been a rush to beat the public transport nightmare that London presented. It might have been the content of the slides. Some might have just needed some fresh air. Jessica had talked to Maryam before the presentation began, advising her that no matter what, she needed to push on to get through the complete content. Maryam had her presentation timed, and she was keeping that time well despite the distractions. For a while, she focused on the Mahant, whose strength she could draw on. She also noticed that, as well as the Hindu group, most of the Christians, Muslims, and Buddhists were still intact.

There was always going to be a fringe element that would protest, but in front of her, still listening, were the leaders of over eighty percent of the world's faithful, and the Jews were still there too.

***

Discussions in the Clouds

As the day drew to a close, Yitzakh was amazed at how much ground they had covered. In the past, these interfaith meetings had been flowery but mostly ineffectual. But this conference had gravitas, well done Oxford. Yitzakh was keen on a lot of the girl's ideas and set himself the arduous task of reading her paper when it was published.

Yitzakh was a man of action, he liked change and he liked change for the better even more.

He was especially keen when she talked about food and water, particularly the repurposing of water. Technology so close to Yitzakh's heart. Israel repurposed 90% of its water, compared to about 4% in the US. He knew they led the world, along with Kuwait and Singapore. Israel was also in an elite group using seventy five percent desalination for drinking water and drawing from only two dams. If other countries could be encouraged to use water the way Israel did, many of the world's water problems would be solved. But it's like anything else, if things are plentiful and the price is low, people will consume them without a thought for their impact now or in the future.

Yitzakh couldn't see who Ari ejected. He just saw his friend move like a sinewy cat from behind the rostrum on an intercept course for something. He thought he should ask him later what had happened. The two of them were going to spend some more time having a drink; it would likely be many years before they would see each other again. Ari really wasn't welcome in Israel; there was leftover bad blood. Yitzakh knew there was bad blood everywhere; somehow they must find a way.

He shot a look over at Hasan and his group, small friendships might just pave the way where the old hatreds crumbled.

* * *

Hasan was thinking through what he had seen.

Bismillah, the amalgamation of faiths would be difficult to sell to the followers of Mohammad. Concessions would be needed even to start talks on the matter. Some surety that this wouldn't become Christian-dominated. He thought carefully about the message Maryam brought. One faith, slowly and methodically guiding governments to make decisions for the betterment of all people.

A wonderful message, maybe he could use the fifth verse of the *surah Al-Alaq*. Some spin on that might get it close. For the rest, he will need help from Allah.

The resource usage was already widely distributed in Muslim countries: Kuwait, Syria, UAE, Oman, Pakistan, Iran, Egypt, and Algeria. The list was extensive. Even in Palestine, if they could stop throwing stones at the Jewish tanks.

But they failed on so many other things. A wasteful elite with too many Ferraris, Bugattis, and McLarens, and somehow the fifth pillar of Islam, the *Haji*, was being used to increase social standing. The rich attended annually, while the poor struggled to make the pilgrimage once in their lifetime. The rich few had five-star hotels attached to the marble outside the grand mosque, lavish banquets, and other luxuries, while some of the poor survive on dry bread and sleep where and when they could while waiting in the sun for prayers. For many, the trip, which was supposed to transcend race, nationality, and economic background, had become a torturous experience.

How do we lobby the government to get the rich to better protect the poor when our endless sermons about the message of the prophet have no effect? Why are people so unwilling to give up such a small amount of their lavish luxuries to allow more equal ground for those who have not been so fortunate? For many, even the fifteen percent the mosque asked for annually was an evasive subject.

Hasan had luxuries, but his hard-fought Mercedes C63 was a far cry from a Bugatti, and many of those faithful had the Bugatti just for Mondays.

Chapter Nine

The Messiah

The path is the path

Something had always been a little different about Boris.

He felt it, others saw it, some commented on it and even more people threw it in his face. But Boris just let them; he had an infinite capacity for forgiveness; it was one of his things.

For who he was destined to become, Boris was born in the strangest of circumstances, as no one predicted. His mother and father were good, hardworking citizens. His mother was Catholic, originally from Belize, and his father was an Anglo-Saxon Anglican. They had a modest house in the London suburb of Barking, just off Longbridge Road. Boris' mother worked at the hospital, and his father tried his hardest to get odd jobs when he could but was mostly unemployed. Boris also had a younger sister, Naina.

You could say he grew up in a perfect nuclear household.

Boris spent his early life looked after almost exclusively by his dad. Then he migrated to six uneventful years at Eastbury Community Primary School and followed that up with another seven equally uneventful years at Eastbury Community School.

He wasn't particularly good at anything, but on the bright side, he wasn't particularly bad at anything.

Boris was bullied excessively but had developed a capacity for forgiveness early, so he never stood up for himself and took no revenge.

That in itself wasn't the reason he didn't attract a strong friendship group, but it was probably a contributing factor. Making friends just wasn't in Boris's DNA. It was a return journey, give and take, a bond, and Boris just hadn't read the same map as everybody else.

At the end of his school life, Boris had good enough scores to go on to college if he wanted to. Maybe not a degree, but the school councillor had suggested he choose something creative, as of all things Boris was mediocre at, he was most pleasingly mediocre at things that he did with his hands. Metalwork, woodwork, and visual art. The councillor had wanted to suggest he do something in the arts, but any art Boris had turned to had been fairly boring in its subject and its interpretation.

He was great at copying other people's stuff.

Well, great is an exaggeration.

He was OK.

So at eighteen, with a family that loved him, very average grades, and minimal prospects, Boris entered college.

He got a position at Barking and Dagenham College doing carpentry. He liked carpentry, but somewhere in the enjoyment he just couldn't come up with a final product that was any good. Midway through the first year, his teacher suggested he try bricklaying as it had good government sponsorship and a guarantee of a job once his study was complete. Boris also wasn't particularly good at bricklaying, but he also wasn't bad, at least not as bad as he was at carpentry, so he stuck at it.After two years of training, Boris passed all his exams and became qualified, but it was the year that an excess of bricklayers also became qualified, for the second year in a row. When Boris finally graduated, there was actually an enormous shortage of carpenters. It seems a large number of people had made the switch to bricklaying as a result of a government initiative to combat inequities in trades and severe tradesman shortages, and now there were not enough jobs for all the new bricklayers.

It was about this time, at the age of 21, that Boris began to feel different. He didn't know why, but he just did. He stopped shaving to start with. He also ditched haircuts and often just had his hair in a mess. He hadn't put on any weight but started wearing very baggy clothing, except his shorts, which he kept skin tight. He spent a lot of time outdoors meditating, which his father called lazing about. The truth was he was engaged in stuff that took some concentration, so it wasn't lazing. After a few years, he had managed to really understand life better and began chastising people on the street about their immoral or poor behaviour. This, of course, led to a number of very severe beatings, but Boris had an infinite capacity for forgiveness, so they were just part of the fabric of his life. His parents tried so hard to intervene; they really were a very loving family. But Boris continued on his path, and so instead of creating any fuss, they supported him where they could and picked him up where they couldn't. More damage control than anything else.

Boris' sister had pretty much given up by the time she got to eighteen.

She had discovered boys who were not Boris. She found herself far more interested in living life, drugs, alcohol, and sex. Lots of sex. Boris didn't need sex, not even with himself. He somehow had developed that niche in life where nobody saw him as useful except himself, and nobody saw him as intelligent except himself.

At one stage, he considered himself invisible, but he wasn't, he was just truly and unequivocally his own person.

Still living at home, things became fairly tense at Boris's house when Naina became pregnant. She didn't really want to say who the father was, or she didn't know. Apparently, at the time, Naina was into a lot of group sex, sometimes just her and a load of boys, sometimes lots of girls and one boy, or more often than not, girls and boys and boys that dressed like girls and boys that wanted to be girls eventually. She was enjoying it all either way until, oops. When little Aeta was born, the two-up, two-down in Barking just got a little more crowded. Boris and Naina had always shared a room, so Aeta just squeezed in there. For anyone who has tried to squeeze a modern western baby in places, it just doesn't happen, but being a loving family, they made do.

Boris spent some of the time sleeping in the living room, and then he slept there most nights. In the summer months, Boris would sleep outdoors, either in the small garden out the back or just on the front porch. A few times, he was quite violently assaulted while sleeping on the front porch. During one attack, the assailants took his keys, went inside, stole the TV and came back for more before Boris's dad came down and chased them off.

Boris actually spent a week in the hospital after that, with a few cracked ribs, some head lacerations, and a particularly characteristic limp. On top of all his other beatings, the hospital took a bit of an interest and ran some tests on Boris. They found that all the beatings over the years had caused some fairly bad brain damage. Not quite enough to affect him outwardly but definitely cause some internal damage, something you might call soft spots. The prognosis just wasn't enough to justify a prolonged stay, so Boris was sent home and scheduled for a checkup in three months.

As that time came and went, Boris' outward appearance consolidated. It didn't really improve, but his beard became slightly less like a bird's nest, and his hair was greased down and smoothed more with dirt and oil than product. It could be said that it actually looked quite fashionable in the era of bold, long beards. Boris had finally grown into his niche.

Pushed out more and more as Aeta grew, Boris had taken more and more time outside.

First, he went to the local Islamic Community Centre, where many of the Muslims thought he must be one of them and were happy for him to just hang out. A lot of the morality he spouted, which was much maligned on the street, actually fit in quite well and was almost in line with the words of the imam. However, Boris wasn't good at sports, games, or even art, so many of the things to do weren't for him, leaving him just hanging in corridors, gardens, or on the edge of sporting games.

After leaving late one night, he ran into a small group of much younger boys from the community centre, who gave him a particularly vicious beating and told him not to come near the place again.

Not to be disheartened, Boris moved to the Christian Centre. First, he asked if he could help out, and to his utter lack of comprehension, they asked him if he could build a small brick wall for them in the garden.

So he did.

It wasn't a very good brick wall, but it was solid and held up well. From this simple act, his reputation grew, and he managed to build a few other walls around the community. People did find him a bit strange, and the Christian community learned to act morally around Boris or expect him to comment.

Only comment, though.

Boris was not known to act; he just judged. His time at the Christian Centre led to some early friendships, although, as with many things in Boris's life, they didn't exactly follow a Disney script.

His early dealings with Jeffrey, Pinka, Jobella, and Whachta were more 'listen, then gob' sessions.

Boris talked, they listened, and then they spat at him. But for the first time, he had what we can loosely call followers.

Time moved on, and more followers joined.

Boris would talk sometimes for a while, but more often than not for a short time, before the group would spit on him incessantly and deride him. His infinite capacity for forgiveness intact, he was happy just to finally be part of a group, and particularly with Watcha and Big X around, there were no more beatings from anyone.

The new guy, Si, had even started telling stories at home to his sister about his interactions with Boris. She used Tik Tok to post a funny video about Boris. As with all other Tik Toks, Si's sister's item was web crawled by an AI news aggregator. The aggregator had noticed the lack of news about religion, even though a lot of people had tagged religion as a point of interest in their news feeds. It couldn't seem to make sense of the Tik Tok, but it noticed the video highlighted the morality lectures of Boris and less about the subsequent treatment of Boris after this.

It was also noted that Si's sister said Boris didn't fight back and, in turn, forgave everyone, which the AI determined to be a religious act.

The whole thing was in a community centre, so it did have some religious overtones.

This particular AI news aggregator ran the story. Across the world, millions of news feeds added Boris to the religious news subject. In the US alone, over a million people opened the article and watched Tik Tok, allowing up to seven advertisements that formed part of the composite web page to credit the tech company that ran the aggregator out of the Estonian Data Centre.

When that aggregator published its results to other trusted aggregators, they all also ran the story and subsequently increased their advertising revenue. Silently, other untrusted aggregators monitored the transactions and joined in to run the story. The first Tik Tok story about Boris had thirty seven million hits across all platforms.

Si's sister freaked.

The next day, she went to the Christian Centre to hang with her big brother. She had never been before, but she alone scored nine million views on her first Tik Tok. This time she wanted to get some footage of Boris direct.

Unfortunately, Boris didn't turn up that day; he was difficult to nail down, so she just asked the others on camera to tell her stuff.

Most of the group were semi-literate, unemployed, obnoxious, and spoke in the riddles of new, revised East London rhyming slang. When she got home, Si's sister had more than enough for ten new Tik Toks, but none of them actually had Boris in them. She posted all ten Tik Toks in the hope that something would stick.

With the exponential increase in content about Boris, some of the AI aggregators thought maybe there was more to Boris than met the eye. Simultaneously, they created a storm of controversy to try to increase advertising revenue, all of them creating words for Boris rather than using any words he might have actually said.

The storm worked, and by the end of the week, Boris had over two hundred million views across all platforms and all media. He had peaked at number two hundred on Google's most searched words.

After wandering for a while but now at home again, Boris had actually slept in the back for the night. It was hot inside, but during the night a howling northerly had swept down the Thames and caught him outside in just his shorts, no blanket, no sheet.

Because of the earlier thieving incident, Boris didn't keep a key with him. He had tried knocking on the door, but the wind was so loud that no one could hear him. By the time his dad came down in the morning, he was freezing and had caught a terrible flu, leaving him stuck in the house for three days feeling particularly bad.

On the third day, he felt better and headed for the Christian Centre.

He thought it surprising that a large number of vans lined the street.

As he got closer, he realised they were news vans.

Something must have happened, maybe a mass shooting.

But no.

They were all looking for him.

***

Not the Garden of Gethsemane

Jessica first heard about Boris on her news feed, as most other followers of religious news had. She had followed the initial link, clicked to allow cookies, minimised the pop-up, and read the article while the video ads auto-played in the background.

"Old Spice, the man your man could smell like," the advertising catch line rang out. Jessica had the sound up quite loud in her office, as she had been playing some Handel, because the mood took her. She looked up and saw Rosemary turn around with her eyebrows raised.

Jessica clicked 'skip ad' but the cheeky button that had said 'skip ad' changed to 'video will play when the ad is finished'.

She almost blasphemed.

Finally, she could take a peaceful moment to read the article. When she started, she was a little interested, but the article really didn't grab her. Some strange bricklayer in Barking is giving morality lessons at the Christian centre. Not really her cup of tea, but she held back from ticking the "Don't show me more like this" box.

Jessica had a lot on her plate.

She had completed a full review of the venue in London. At first, they said the venue was a five hundred-seat auditorium, but it turns out it is actually an eight hundred-seat auditorium, and they were just going to block off the back five rows. She thought it looked big when she was there.

To her, that would make the place look almost a third empty, which is just not the way religious people like it. You must really have not enough seats and people standing at the back or more people. She had confirmation from just about everyone. Fifty Catholics, fifty in her own Anglican delegation, fifty from the various Orthodox, thirty Methodists, thirty Presbyterians, thirty Protestants, and fifteen Baptists making up two hundred and twenty-five Christians. She had a few other fringe turn-ups: Seventh-day Adventists, LDS Mormons, and Scientologists, but they were in groups of less than five.

So let's say two fifty tops.

The two main Muslim groups had fifty each, so that was another one hundred for them. The Hindus had fifty people for each of the main three denominations and then another twenty-five for the fringe. So that would get it up to one hundred and seventy-five for them. From there, the Buddhists said there were twenty or thirty in each group plus the Dalai Lama's group, so that's one hundred.

The Buddhists were a bit airy-fairy; she was nervous.

How was she going to fill those last two hundred seats?

She thought about all the so-called "folk religions."

A number of them had London or Paris headquarters. How do I accommodate them all? Many of them are on the fringe of true religious organisations and would be unlikely to answer any call for change. Part of the reason they are where they are is that they couldn't compromise with a wider group, so they split off to have it their way.

Sure, later, once this new entity is underway and signed off by the big four or five, maybe we can hold meetings with them and give them a bit of a franchise statement, allowing them to join, so to speak. But involving them in this meeting seemed like a stretch. Maybe some Baha'is, Jehovah's Witnesses, Taoists, Shintos, and Rastafarians she had contact with from previous interfaith meetings She fired off an email, including all the contact details, to Rosemary to follow up.

It was late notice, but they would come and be happy to be involved. It was rare that the mainstream called on the fringe; they would come for curiosity's sake.

Jessica asked Rosemary to come in, and efficiently, as always, Rosemary turned and came in with a pad of paper and pen in hand, ready to do the bishop's bidding.

"We have Tom coming to our interfaith meeting." He's going to do the opening."

Jessica was visibly shaking. "I got the call in the car. He is 100% confirmed."

"Yeah, yeah, yeah." Rosemary started doing circle work in the bishop's office.

"Woop, woop, woop!" she hooted.

"I can't believe it," Jessica said. "Dalai Lama, the King, and now Tom."

"We should get Boris too." Rosie said flippantly.

Jessica stopped celebrating and looked quizzically at Rosemary.

"Who exactly is Boris?" Jessica asked, "I just saw him on my news feed."

"Yes, he's on all the news feeds now, and on the TV."

Jessica turned on the TV in her office.

ITV, Boris.

BBC. Boris.

Channel 4. Big Brother Repacked.

Sky. Boris.

"Wow. Three out of four channels." Jessica exclaimed. "That's not bad coverage!"

"Apparently he just keeps saying seriously meaningful stuff and getting beaten up for it, but just keeps saying it and forgiving people."

Rosemary seemed like she knew what she wanted to say but couldn't get her words organised.

"They are saying he's the next big thing religiously. But no one can get an interview; it seems he's a bit camera shy."

"Indeed." Jessica fostered a small thought.

"Thank you, Rosemary. Any chance we can get Boris's number?"

"I can only try Bishop," said Rosemary as she scuttled off to her desk.

A while later, Rosemary knocked on Jessica's open door. "Sorry, Bishop, no luck with a phone number for Boris." She had a list of possibilities all scrubbed out.

"Last chance is that he hangs out at the Manor Park Christian Centre on High St. North. I tried to call them, but the switchboard has been jammed all day."

"Thanks, Rosemary. I can get there in less than two hours if I get some luck on the M25. I will be out the rest of the day."

Luck should never be used in the same sentence as the M25 without a negative connotation. Jessica had never liked it, and she was not alone. Often nicknamed Europe's biggest car park, it has four lanes each way of misguidance, misdirection, and misfortune. The truth is, she had an option, but it currently showed an extra twenty minutes to go on the A406, and she would hit London around lunchtime, so the M25 was probably safer.

Google Maps agreed, and so it was.

Around two hours later, after minimal traffic and, some might say, intervention from above, Jessica was moving her S6 down Romford Road towards High St. North. The difference between this area of London and the town area in Oxford was stark. The Middle Eastern influence was strong, and for some reason, the whole high street was about food and cars.

The traffic became heavier as she approached High St., but then released as she turned the corner. High St. flowed quickly, and as she pulled over the railway bridge, she noticed the chippy on the left had fifty people grouped around it, presumably waiting for food.

The whole area was a sea of people.

Jessica pulled up in front of the Manor Park Christian Centre and saw nowhere to park. Sometimes you can be lucky and they have a spot for the minister, vicar, or priest, but in this case, nothing.

She kept driving and noticed a spare parking space down one of the side streets. Only five minutes of parking, but it would do for her to look up her ace in the hole. She pulled out her mobile phone and used Google Maps to track down the nearest Anglican Church, which was an eight-minute walk away.

She had time.

Parking at the church, she popped her head inside the office and saw the local minister.

"Bishop of Oxford," she said, "just popping round the corner on church business. I was hoping I could use your car park for a bit."

The old minister was very surprised. A bishop from Oxford at his church.

"Yes, of course. I don't have a car," he said, "but the station is right there, and traffic is choking at the best of times." She waved at him as she walked out, not waiting for the conversation to blossom.

Jessica made her way down Romford Road past Woodgrange Park Tube and up Salisbury Road back to High Street.

As she walked along past the two-up, two-down houses, she was reminded how much of England lived this way, a far cry from the expanse Oxford offered. Out in front of one of the houses, Jessica noticed that a child had been drawing with chalk on the road.

Pictures of animals, two by two, with a slogan at the top in blue: 'Noah's Ark. God First'.

To her dismay, presumably another child had crossed out God and written in green, replacing the word 'God' with the word 'Planet'.

"They are into the children," she said under her breath. "We are in so much trouble."

As she crossed the rail bridge, she noticed a small group of people gathered. One of them was standing in the centre, doing what could only be called orating.

Could it be?

She circled around, past all the TV people at the chippy, and along the curve of Bluebelle Avenue.

There on the grounds of the Fairbairn Boxing Club, being spat on, was Boris.

She waited for the group to disperse. Boris had taken a seat on the park bench. He looked quite pleased with himself, if not a little oblivious to the gaggle of news people just metres away.

"How are you Boris?" Jessica was to the point as always: "I am the Bishop of Oxford. Any chance we can have a private chat?"

"Sure," he said.

"Did those boys just spit on you?" Jessica noticed large globules of saliva hanging off Boris' head and his jacket.

"A little," he said. "It's their way; I don't judge them for it."

"Well, that is big of you," Jessica said. "A little unhygienic, but in this day and age, the way people show affection does beggar belief."

"We all have our crosses to bear, right?" Boris said philosophically.

"What were you saying to them to make them spit on you?" Jessica was truly curious.

"I was telling them how the judgement was here and that for their actions, everyone would be held accountable." Boris looked out across the small playground to a point beyond where the railway line snaked away.

"Who is doing the judging Boris?" Jessica asked.

"I am returned to judge on behalf of our father. That is my place before I join him again at his right hand."

Jessica stopped and looked at Boris.

He was such an ordinary character; nothing stood out to make him any different from the next man. His hair and beard were almost unkempt, his clothes were baggy, and she might say they were quite dull. Jessica wasn't hugely interested in fashion, but she thought perhaps that was the way it was done today. Boris had so many bruises and scars from where he had been battered over the years.

"You look like you take quite a hiding, Boris. How are you judging?"

"I don't hold that against them. I forgive their acts of frustration with me. Sometimes what I have to say is difficult even for me to hear. I might beat me up too, given half a chance."

Jessica smiled, just short of a laugh.

What a character!

"What do you think about the news people and what they are saying?"

"They will be judged most harshly." Boris had a very straight face. "Their intentions are not pure; they are clouded by greed, pride, and gluttony."

"Can you help them Jessica? You radiate faith, hope, and charity."

"I can only try," Jessica said. She pondered how Boris had picked up her name.

"The effort brings a kinder judgement than the result." Boris looked at her directly.

Jessica was dumbfounded.

Who is this guy?

"Do you know who I am Jessica?" Boris asked, "Will anybody really recognise me if they see me? Is anyone really looking?"

"We live in a world of images Boris." Jessica agreed, "images that distract from the truth, not ones that enhance it."

Jessica didn't want to answer his first question.

"So am I less real because I don't fit the mould?" Boris was distracted as another small group of local boys gathered around. Jessica turned and saw them too.

"No, Boris, you are real. Why don't you come with me to the local church? I have someone I would like you to meet."

"OK Jessica," Boris had never been so agreeable.

Jessica and Boris walked back to All Saints Anglican Church. The walk was done in silence. Once there, she explained to the old priest that she was running a convention here in London and wanted Boris to come. The old priest had seen

Boris around and had once helped him home after being beaten so badly he could barely walk.

"He seems a good lad," the priest said. "I will look after him."

"Thank you, Father." Jessica had to make it back to Oxford tonight, so with the clock ticking, she gave the priest her number and asked for him to call.

About anything.

"Try not to take what he says too much to heart, OK?" Her final words to the priest were prophetic in their own right.

"I'll get him there in two days." The priest confirmed, "I'll let his folks know he's here with me so they don't worry."

***

No-one believed then, why would they believe now

Boris had been sitting in the audience listening.

The kindly father at All Saints had delivered him as promised. He had been seated at the back of a strange group of people from folk religions. Most were good-natured and thoughtful, but he read in the hearts of many, too much greed, too much pride, and way way too much lust, gluttony, and surprisingly sloth.

On the first day, Boris just watched and listened.

Tom was inspiring; Boris saw into his heart and saw the conflict, the beauty, and the ambition. There was nothing cardinal in the sins of Tom except a little pride, but the truth was that it was authentic pride, and Tom managed it well given his notable gifts and his ridiculous bank balance.

The rest of day one seemed like a blur to Boris; everyone seemed to know some-one else. As they met each other again, renewing old acquaintances, lost briefly but now allowed to be recaptured with the decline of interest in COVID-19.

Boris knew nobody, but it turned out everybody knew who he was. They pointed and whispered; most of what they said was not complimentary.

Some made comments that he thought he was the second coming. Boris mostly kept his thoughts to himself until the Bishop of Oxford asked him how he was, and then he told her.

"What a collection Jessica!" he sighed.

"Yes," she replied, "this is the vanguard of the faith, Boris. The best and the brightest."

"Well, it's not." he stated. "It's mostly just the senior people. A junket to London was on offer; they had to take it." Jessica was actually not shocked by Boris's words.

"Some are good, strong, loyal, and well-meaning. But many of the best and brightest are actually pinned down by people such as these. These people find themselves old and terrified of the energy of youth, so all they can do is fight to hold on to what power they have by whatever means. For many of them, those are lies; for some, I can see in their hearts, wrath."

Now that caught Jessica's attention. "Wrath Boris?" she queried.

"Many in our midst have sanctioned murder previously Jessica," Boris said with sadness. "Our father will not greet them openly."

Jessica still wasn't sure what to make of Boris. She knew anyone could make that statement based on reading the guest list and the newspaper.

"For a second time, they just can't believe it's true when presented with what they preach." Boris's words fell easily, like petals on the wind.

Jessica pondered.

She had previously read a survey that showed that about forty percent of Americans believe that Jesus is likely to return by 2050. The number varied when put to different faiths, including fifty eight percent of white evangelical Christians, thirty two percent of Catholics, and twenty seven percent of white mainline Protestants. According to the Catholic Church, the second coming will happen in a single moment, suddenly and unexpectedly. Not even the angels, saints, or demons know when it will occur. It will cause the fullness of the reign of God and the consummation of the universe and mankind.

"How do we convert faith into truth, Jessica?" Boris's words were not helping, and she could again see why he was beaten up so often.

The truth is that Jessica was a living personification. She turned faith into action. She allowed people to openly see in her life the very evidence of such faith at work. Jessica was a living witness to the faith that she believed in and an open expression of compassion towards others. Through her service, Jessica spent her life converting her faith into truth.

"Jessica, can I have a word?" She heard from behind her.

She could see the archbishop with his hand in the air, waving it like he needed the lavatory.

"Excuse me, Boris, it's the boss." Jessica said as she moved away.

Sadly, she didn't get to talk to Boris again. The kindly priest collected him on day one and looked after him, ready for the next day. Early on the second day, Boris admonished one of the other delegates for a poor-form comment about the Dalai Lama, something about a widely covered media article on an indiscretion. Boris noted the pureness of the Dalai Lama's spirit and the way he treated his fellow man; even though he wielded enormous power and influence, he used them only for good. Boris took umbrage when one of the people seated nearest to him uttered some derogatory comments under his breath. A small, rather heated discussion broke out in the area between Boris and three other unrelated delegates, but no one spat on Boris, so he was happy enough to just take his seat and continue to watch. One of the other delegates was not happy and mentioned it to security, who passed it on to Ari.

Normally Ari would accompany Tom everywhere, but Tom was going back to Croatia and wanted Ari to wrap this up first before joining him. Ari had seen that Yitzakh was here, so he was happy to stay on. The two of them had enjoyed some time last night on trips down memory lane. Ari had even managed to convince Yitzakh to enjoy a few drinks. Yitzakh had not many; Ari had a few more. Not enough to give him a hangover, but just regret that he didn't get on the plane with Tom and leave this to the local guys. At least he could enjoy another drink with Yitzakh later if he could tear him away from the other Jews.

Boris continued to sit.

Later in the afternoon, Maryam made her presentation.

While others looked on at Maryam's work, Boris focused on the girl. In contrast to the Dalai Lama, Maryam was a very young soul, no less pure, but, you might say, naive. Things got heated as the speech reached a conclusion, and many of the people around him stood and hurled insults. First, they were aimed at Maryam, which Boris could not abide by; he chastised people openly. Then, in the midst of his chastising, some old feuds were reignited as delegates began hurling abuse at other delegates. Most of it was between fractured factions, hurling abuse at others that had remained true to the original teachings of this prophet or another. Some more personal comments aimed at delegates' personal lives. Boris heard one comment about sexual misconduct but looked into the heart of the abuser and saw they were, in fact, the perpetrator and were accusing to deflect the blame. Here in a public forum. Boris stood up and tried to silence the fracas with an almighty roar.

"You shall not judge. That is the role my father has bestowed on me. It is my burden to bear. This time without the forgiveness or compassion I showed last time."

The room hadn't stopped. It turns out Boris's loudest voice just wasn't enough competition for the seasoned orators in the room. Boris raised himself up, as he never had before; his infinite ability to forgive was gone; it was just not appropriate amongst these men who claimed to represent God on earth. He moved to the end of his row and began to walk down the aisle towards the rostrum.

"Each of you listen! I have looked into your hearts and found you wanting. There was time for you to rectify your sins. But this will only come through actions; there is no one left to take your confession."

Ari had positioned himself close to the stage. It gave him the best view of the whole room. The noise hadn't worried him; he was from Tel Aviv, and the noise wasn't anything as loud as market night. When he saw Boris get up, he tensed. He had already received one complaint against this kid. He had checked, and the kid wasn't affiliated with any known religion and was one of the 'special guests' the bishop had added last minute. He had let her know they were a security risk, but the bishop needed to fill seats. Tom liked full seats, so Ari let it swing. Ari was no longer going to let it swing.

When Boris started his move down towards the rostrum, Ari acted. He calculated a cut-off point, signalled to his two other security team members in the auditorium to come in from left and right, and moved at a pace so all three would converge on Boris simultaneously. They wrapped him up in seconds and had him out the main door in equal time. Efficient, silent, and lethal. That was why Tom paid the big money.

Once outside, they threw Boris to the ground and kicked him a few times for good measure. Boris looked up at Ari but didn't say anything. He could see in his heart that Ari was not a good man, but he was a man with a purpose, some might say a warped intention. Ari took a moment to aim a kick at Boris, just seconds after one of the other security guards also kicked Boris particularly hard in the back. Boris had been forced to bend up, leaving his head exposed to Ari's final shot.

Unconscious and unwanted, Ari and his team left Boris in the alley to rot and headed back inside to protect the conference.

Chapter Ten

The Zealot

Maryam had settled into her hotel room for the night.

She was a very neat and orderly person and always took the time before she slept to store or tidy those things left over from the day, and organise things for the next day.

Along with her faith, it was her ritual.

She was pondering the day and the way these highly educated theologians viewed her vision. Many with the open eyes that they should. Some with closed hearts, looking for a selfish future based on a compromised past.

Too many personalities, too many differences, and such a focus on those differences.

Maryam thought that the One God should be an easy concept, you may say the simplest of all concepts. You have a single all-powerful, all-knowing, all-seeing entity that handles everything. There is no variation, no committee, and no discussion.

His way, or the spiritual highway.

So the problem then becomes the interpretation of whatever words or signs are offered, and who is interpreting them?

Catholics had done it over centuries with the sword and various other sharp implements, stretching devices, and pots of very hot liquids. Buddhists had let it go and tried to be nice to others. Hindus had just created more gods to fill any gaps; and Islam had taken a similar path to the Catholics to gain ground, but held that ground by creating a sense of community and belonging.

With a clean slate, Maryam had no doubt her plan would be the best for humanity, but the luxury of a clean slate had long passed as all the faiths had history between them.

History that was long, dark, and, in most cases, very violent.

She thought about the lovely Buddhists she met today. Shining lights, peaceful, venerable, but the history of Buddhism hasn't always been so, and it was similar venerable people that either instigated, condoned, or even justified violence.

The delegation from Myanmar actually had a shocking human rights reputation, but they looked like wizened old masters.

What was she to think?

The lovely imam from London was such a caring, empathetic individual, and yet he stood on the shoulders of shocking atrocities against other religions and, if the history books are to be believed, even against people of his own faith.

If power corrupts, then how does inherited power corrupt through generations?

Maryam did not leave her own faith out of her thoughts. She knew of the shocking acts perpetrated against minorities, especially Muslims, by those in her own country, as religious leaders both in and out of politics did nothing in denial or gave tacit approval to such violent actions.

Maryam honestly believed in her heart that they all prayed to the same god. She called him Vishnu; Jews called him Yahweh; and Muslims called him Allah. Everyone had a name, but some others couldn't see past the name to discover the similarities.

Maryam wondered at how fast the security took down and removed one of the delegates.

When she first saw him move towards the rostrum, she thought he was defending her. She hoped that delegate was alright.

Still lost in her thoughts she opened the door to her room. She needed a snack and remembered that the vending machine in the lobby had nut bars.

Perfect.

She went down the stairs. The hotel lobby had its usual throng of very dodgy-looking people. Not wanting to engage anyone, she solicited a nut bar from the machine quickly before heading back upstairs.

Maryam used her card on the door and moved inside. She waited for the familiar click of the door meeting the latch, but it never came. She turned to see a man in her room, one of the aforementioned dodgy-looking men who frequent the lobby.

"Uhhmm, yes." she said stupidly.

"Maryam," he said. Maryam wanted to scream, but fear caught her voice and held it captive, leaving her only with a grunt.

"Uhuh." she replied monotonically.

Fear had now mushroomed into terror.

She was going to be raped; she hadn't known any lovers yet, and this animal was going to take those most joyous of moments from her and her future husband.

"Heretic Maryam!" His eyes narrowed, and he took some straps from his pocket.

Maryam finally broke free of the fear that gripped her and tried to scream, but he was too quick and covered her mouth, embracing her in an iron grip. She was a fighter and tried every trick she knew to break his hold, but he was too big and too strong. He bound her quickly with the straps and sat her unceremoniously on the bed.

"I was at your little presentation today; you think you're so clever, don't you?"

Maryam struggled a little. She was bound and gagged and so couldn't answer. Without an option she just sat and listened.

"At first, I was interested. A sum to end all human suffering."

Maryam noticed he was clearly drugged quite heavily, either with newly taken drugs or with drugs he had been consuming over a long period of time.

"Have you ever known suffering?" He let the words hang over her like a noose that he was going to use.

"I thought not, so I said to myself that if she knew suffering, maybe she would be better able to comment on its cause and its cure. I thought I would come to show you."

Fear was not an emotion that was easily gauged.

No matter how frightened you were, you could always appear to achieve a heightened level of dread. Fear could rise and fall exponentially, or linearly, forming pirouettes up and dissolving into white-knuckle rides down. This was the journey Maryam was now on, and for her, this was her first excursion with many of these emotions.

"I imagined while I watched you on the stage what you would look like bound up like a pig, as I cut you, to watch you bleed as the people you casually discussed in your presentation bleed." He pulled an apple out of his jacket and a large Bowie knife from a sheath he had secured to his back.

Maryam blacked out.

He slapped her quite hard and spat in her face. "Wake up, bitch. You will feel this."

Groggily, she came to, and her dread resumed its journey.

"Well, I won't be doing that," he said, taking a large bite of the apple.

"I stole it from the reception," he said. "Some idiot had left a whole bunch of fruit in a bowl on the floor." She watched him peel off the sticker that had gotten caught in his teeth. The apple was a special apple for Buddhist prayer. She took a moment to ask Buddha for guidance, then admonished herself and gave a similar prayer to Vishnu.

"So, then I watched your little presentation for a bit longer."

It was clear to Maryam that even before he became gripped in the arms of whatever drug had him, he wasn't well educated. She guessed he had barely completed middle school. His speech impediment might have been the reason; it was minor and could be fixed , if not with therapy, possibly with minor surgery. What a different path life might have taken for him if someone had spent the time to make that change early in his life. She guessed the long healed scars on his face and his forearms were from beatings. His father, maybe other children, maybe other drug users, or maybe just a long litany of beatings from all those people.

"It probably belongs to those yellow-robed numpties." he spat. "Stupid priests are all the same."

He continued to monologue as Maryam's fear continued to bound around her brain with reckless abandon.

"I've had my fair share of priests. Dirty, filthy buggers, say the word of God is peace, the word of God is love, and the word of God is forgiveness, then shove a purple-headed cock up your arse."

Maryam could only guess that that pain occurred many years ago. It would be hard to imagine one of the small, thin men she had met in the last few days overpowering this behemoth.

"Hate them," he seemed lost in his own memory. For a moment Maryam did feel his pain, and in her own mind, she felt sorry for him and hoped his soul could find a better path in the next world.

"Then I saw that all this you were proposing was actually about birth control. So there are more people like you and fewer people like me. Well, that choice 'ain't yours, 'ain't anyone's."

Maryam's eyes widened in terror, and he looked at her directly; he almost looked through her. His eyes were bloodshot, full of pain and anger. She let out a small gasp from beneath the binding that held her mouth closed.

"That offends my God," he said. "The God of Life."

Even though they were so tightly bound together, Maryam might have just let a little bit of water slip out from between her legs. Her terror must have finally reached a crescendo.

"Is this it then?" He turned and picked up her thesis, which she had piled so neatly on the hotel desk.

Maryam hated reading on the computer screen, so she printed a copy this afternoon at a printer in London. To her horror, she realised the printed copy and the three backups on her laptop were the only complete copies of her thesis. She meant to fix the cloud backup error on her laptop but hadn't, as she had been busy, so the cloud copy was a good three months old. With all the fuss over this conference, she hadn't sent a copy to her PhD supervisor for over a month. The only copies anyone else had were the smaller version on a USB stick with the swami and an even more dumbed-down version she shared with the Bishop of Oxford.

Her life's work was laid open and bare in front of her, with a madman pawing maliciously at the edges.

"Is this where you write it all?" He picked up the laptop and dropped it hard on the floor.

Maryam flinched but thanked her luck that she had been able to afford a solid-state drive that could survive such force. If he raped her and left, she could recover what she needed from that.

Clearly not as uneducated as she may have surmised, he picked up the broken laptop and used his knife to open the back. With a knowledgeable eye, he used it to stab through the hard drive and through the desk. The knife was left to sit like the 'Lance of Longinus' while he continued his mayhem elsewhere.

"I hope you have a backup," he grinned, doing a little dance.

He moved back to the desk and took up the metal bin that sat next to it. Placing it in front of where Maryam sat, he dangled her thesis in her face.

He ripped out five random pages and lit them using his cigarette lighter before throwing the pages unceremoniously into the bin.

"Oops, I nearly burned myself."

Maryam's sadness was etched on her face. She mourned the burned pages, and seeing him tear out another five pages and repeat the ritual, she lamented a future in a world without her guidance.

The smoke choked Maryam.

She hoped, in a small twist of fate, that if he continued, it might set off the smoke alarms in the room. She looked up optimistically at the smoke alarm, wishing the alarm had been tested and that it was correctly powered. The red light blinked a silent confirmation at her, and she sighed, returning her eyes to her assailant.

Unfortunately for Maryam, he had followed her eyes. He lifted his large, calloused right hand and landed it hard on the right side of her face with an almighty slap.

"Nice try, bitch. I'll burn it later." he chided, rolling the remainder of the thesis and stuffing it in his jacket.

"Time we got to the fun stuff." He grunted to Maryam's prevailing terror. He released one of the bindings and cut the front of her nightshirt away, exposing her breasts as they had never been revealed before.

"Let's start with this," he said maniacally, carving a rough-hued Islamic crescent replete with a single star into her right breast. Maryam's muted scream might have sounded like a scream of passion if anyone had been able to hear it. In her head, the scream was deafening. Through the dense pain, she tried to imagine his life: 'Islamic,' she thought, 'I never would have picked that.'

"You think you're so clever, don't you? Well, not so clever now." Maryam was about to faint again but fought through it, remembering the swift pain of the last wake-up she got.

"Always try to prove God wrong or prove you are better than God. Well, now I am the hand of God. How clever do you feel now?" His obviously rhetorical question resounded in Maryam's brain. She thought, 'I was not clever enough to secure my door.'

He cocked a fist with his left hand and punched Maryam hard on her left cheek. The pain was blinding, her vision a dazzling array of purple fractals, yellow stripes, and red dots.

He took the opportunity to carve a cross into her right breast as she lay semi-conscious.

"Now you have some God in your heart." he hissed.

"If you had God in your heart, maybe you wouldn't come up with such crap." He pulled the thesis out of his jacket and pushed the butt of the rolled-up paper hard under her nose. The binding around her mouth staunched the flow of blood slightly, but still, some of it managed to run persistently into her mouth.

"You non-religious academic types are all the same," he continued. "You forget that without God, you are nothing, and we are all nothing."

"Wait!" Maryam cried, but unfortunately, the bindings were so tight that her cries just sounded like a mouse in the final grip of the zinc phosphide poison. "I am Hindu. I am religious," she said, her stifled whimper rising and falling like snow on the wind.

"Why should I give up my right, my God-given right, to have children? For you!" Maryam wanted to plead with him that she understood, but her bindings weren't there to allow a two-way conversation.

She was bleeding a lot and feeling very thin.

She looked more closely at him through what remained of her closing left eye; her right eye was already closed from the earlier punch to the face. He was likely from a migrant family in a large city to the north of the UK. From his look, he could have been Spanish, French, Italian, Greek, or any other Southern mixed race. Definitely some North African influence, but possibly Caribbean as well. His face was the archetypal homogenisation of humanity.

To her horror, he then carved a left-facing Swastika into the right side of her stomach. A left-facing Swastika or Sauvastika. Not the Nazi right-facing one, but left-facing, in Hinduism, symbolising night or the Kaali, the doomsday god. How could he know? He doesn't look that clever. Maybe he just made a mistake and meant to do a Nazi Swastika.

"Alright," he exclaimed, "you are now a work of art." He spat hard on her face, a large, smelly, oozing piece of saliva that now formed part of her face, unyielding and unmoving.

Maryam fainted again. The gyrating nosedive her fear was in turned left and then right, over and under, in an acrobatic display. She was fragile beyond any frailty she had experienced before, bloodless but somehow still bleeding.

"The hand of God is nearly done, princess; don't leave me yet.

He carved a very rough Dharma wheel into the left side of her stomach.

"Now that you have a full set, you do look like a picture."

Whatever drugs he was on were clearly not wearing off, Maryam thought. Unless he is ever without the drugs a madman.

He leaned back to appreciate his work and said, "Room for one more."

On her forehead, he ended with a perfect star of David.

Maryam couldn't see the last inscription and never got the chance as he ran his Bowie knife from one ear to the other, slitting her throat. She felt the clammy liquid ooze down her neck. It was warm; the room was swimming with sweat, smoke, and the smell of blood, but for the first time during this ordeal, she felt at peace.

The pain had subsided, and her fear had morphed into resignation.

In her dying thoughts, Maryam considered his comments. Apparently, everyone was entitled to them, but that didn't give everyone the right to enforce them. That right was most commonly reserved for the weakest of souls, often paired with the strongest of hearts.

With her final breath, in that final light, Maryam saw the irony. In his strong attachment to the right to life, whoever her assailant was, he just didn't feel the same way about murder.

It seems he felt strongly that it was his God-given right to dish out death to those who upset his delicate feelings.

Chapter Eleven

One small step for man, one giant leap backwards...

The police were on site early, scrupulously scrutinising the curious throng of foreign delegates at the conference.

In the early moments, many of their questions were directed to the Bishop of Oxford and to Ari, as the head of security. They wanted a list of everyone who was an attendee and to get everybody's whereabouts after they had left the conference between the hours of 5 p.m. and around 2 a.m. The logistics of that were a nightmare and would take up time the bishop just didn't have. The police were very sensitive to the fact that the King was due to arrive to speak, and so they agreed to take the list and follow up with all the individuals later in the afternoon or in the coming days. They had asked for no one to leave the country, which of course was preposterous as a large number of the international guests had flights booked for that afternoon, that night, or the following day. The police inspector eyed many of the foreign pilgrims suspiciously; a few of the men in robes he even thought he recognised.

King Charles had been in the car on the way to the conference when the tragedy of the night was conveyed to him. His office had placed a call to Jessica, saying that with the events of the previous night, he would now have to distance himself from this tragedy and this conference. In case you haven't followed the life of Charles, he had experienced more than his fair share of tragedy and really needed to leave others to lift from their end for a while.

So, without the King, the Archbishop of Canterbury stepped in to open the last day of the conference. He was a very wise and knowledgeable individual who had a lifetime of experience with grief, so Jessica felt sure that he would handle himself expertly even at such short notice.

Jessica was going to cancel the whole day, but the Archbishop encouraged her to stay the course with a quick rendition from the chorus of Queen's 'The Show Must Go On.'

Jessica was in total shock.

She had put so much effort into this meeting and believed that something needed to come out of it.

She had just felt so bad for Maryam. That beautiful soul.

When she was called by the police in the early morning, she was incredulous. They hadn't needed her to come in and had told her they would be at the conference; it was more of a courtesy call. Her first call was to Marcus to tell him what had happened and confirm that he would still be OK to proceed. He had been in the audience on Day Two, so he knew what Maryam had presented and the chaos it caused. His job was to show them how they could do it. Marcus sounded very groggy but said he would be there. She was very anxious by the time the archbishop took the rostrum.

He seemed quite happy that he was just going to sort of wing it, but she was not.

"Good morning, delegates," he began brightly. "Well, less of the good and more of the morning, I suppose, is a better way of framing it under such tragic circumstances." He took a moment to collect some momentum.

"What a bright light has been snatched from within our midst." He paused again in a lovely, touching moment.

"Who is to blame, we may ask?" He again paused, making Jessica squirm just a touch.

"I suppose we all are," he continued, "not pointing fingers at any particular faith but pointing a collective finger at the failures of faith in general."

He continued quickly as more than just Jessica began to squirm. "Here we sit, keepers of the keys of the word of God, and yet we often spend this time pandering to royalty, at the beck and call of the elite and pacifiers of the masses, and all for what?"

Another pause, this time to accentuate his rhetorical question.

"I say for little if we cannot pacify those out there enough to stop such a heinous act from falling in our midst." Jessica sighed. The archbishop was a master at silence and paused again.

"So where do we turn now?" Jessica felt the archbishop might possibly have nailed this. A short intro she asked for, and that time was drawing near.

"Our faith is compromised; we need to take account and draw in quiet contemplation from the actions of yesterday and think through the legacy of what that beautiful shining light of a girl was trying to tell us. Was she trying to introduce Communism to us, or to question our morality, or our history?" Many of the delegates nodded solemnly, perhaps to the interpretations of the archbishop's words or perhaps just to the feeling that everyone wanted to agree.

"No, of course not." The Archbishop continued as several delegates peered listlessly into nowhere, looking for redemption.

"She was in fact trying to make us forget the past and the inequities of history. She was young and vibrant, just interested in a future that would allow us all to share in the bounty of God's light. Whatever manifestation you may place your faith in, whatever culture you may come from, whatever your social status, whatever personal demons you need to overcome." he fired a glance at the Catholic contingent and then, realising he had done this, moved quickly to the Muslims, then onto the Jews, before feeling very embarrassed and focusing on the Dalai Lama, knowing he must be truly beyond such things.

"So today, Delegates, we need to come together as one, not just to mourn Maryam but to give her brilliance light, and continue the good work she set out. Today, my friends, we need to be united in our resolve to arrive at an outcome that will put aside our petty differences and focus on our common bond. Today, my brothers and sisters in faith, we must be committed to an end that will be for the betterment of humanity."

Jessica was shocked.

The archbishop was truly inspiring, and all of it was off the cuff.

Amazing.

"So, you may ask, what do we need to deliver us closer to the completion of this undertaking?" Several of the delegates looked around at others close to them; there was some shoulder shrugging and some hands raised. The Presbyterian representatives even took it upon themselves to begin discussing what to do.

"A good question it would be. But one already answered, Because, as we all know, if we ask, the good Lord will provide."

The head of the Presbyterian group patted the air in front of his face in a motion to quiet his charges.

"Today we are to be joined by one of the top marketing gurus from the USA."

The Hindu contingent cringed uneasily. Many of them disliked the western use of the term guru for someone who was considered highly knowledgeable in their line of work just through some successful expertise in that field alone.

"He was a shed salesman for many years." The archbishop now appeared to be reading from some flash cards. Jessica wished she had taken a moment to review them and potentially edit out facts that weren't required for this group. "Building what I understand was the biggest shed installation organisation in the United States of America through innovation in inbound and outbound content." The archbishop read the last six words slowly, so the audience, perhaps not familiar with these terms, could easily digest what they meant.

"Now, he is a marketing *blogger*." The archbishop accentuated the word blogger like it was a foreign word to him: "a highly sought-after international keynote speaker who is known for his unique ability to excite, engage, and motivate audiences with his simple yet powerful transformational business approach. Author of the content marketing guidebook 'They Questioned, You Told' and a genuinely lovely man. I would like to introduce Mr Marcus Davenport."

Marcus was wearing a traditional blue suit with a buttoned-up single-breasted jacket and a perfectly starched white shirt; his matching blue pattern tie showed style beyond the comprehension of his audience. He strode confidently to the podium and shook the Archbishop by the hand, and to the shock of the gathered group, he put his hand on the Archbishop's shoulder Probably as a sign of friendship but which came off very disrespectfully. It was almost like he was leading the archbishop from the podium to a nice chair in the sun with a cup of tea.

Jessica was now a little more restless; she hadn't spent any time with Marcus at all during the conference, and he was now her great white hope. She felt the audience waver ever so slightly.

"Thank you, archbishop. What a wonderful introduction! Unique. I have never heard such poignant words in the face of such overwhelming collective grief."

Marcus took a moment to adjust the small wireless microphone attached to the second button of his shirt, creating a loud, booming sound throughout the auditorium.

"Apologies, just settling in some of the equipment," he almost stuttered. "I would like to apologise in advance should I make any technical blunders. None of this AV equipment is mine, and while it is similar, I am not completely familiar with it, so if I go off track, I will need to call on some technical support."

Jessica realised with horror that she had not organised any technical support and quickly fired off an email to the venue to see if they had anyone on site or close by who could assist if needed.

Marcus continued.

"Right. My name is Marcus Davenport, and as the Archbishop so beautifully said, I was a shed salesman." He paused to let that sink in. "In a little less than nine years, I transformed my regional shed business into the largest shed installation company in the US."

Another very short pause, like he was looking for the next chapter in his own CV.

"From there, I pivoted to start Sales Leopard, a company that helped other companies fulfil their potential through marketing and sales strategy. For the last five years, I have been a partner and keynote speaker at QUAKE, one of the most successful digital sales and marketing agencies in the country."

A few delegates looked around. Which country was that? Did he mean the UK, or the US?

"Today I am going to be running quickly through the key points of Maryam's amazing thesis with a particular mind to some possible ways forward and the potential message we will be putting out as a group."

Marcus was not just 'in' marketing. Marcus was truly a bona fide marketing expert. Over the last two days, he felt he had become very closely aligned with this group and could hammer out a solution that they would all get on board with.

"A little caveat before we start: this is not 'THE' way; it's 'A' way. I would like this to be interactive, so if you have any questions, please raise your hand and we will get to it while we are moving along." Marcus moved his left foot slightly to the left to take up a stance.

"So, we have five principles in marketing. Product, price, promotion, place, and people." Marcus switched from a large picture of himself on the presentation screen to the five principles.

"I will make this less of a Marketing 101 lesson and more relevant," he said, switching to the next slide quickly.

"In your case, the product is faith, the price is our eternal souls, the promotion is the most amazing job of weaving yourselves into the fabric of society ever, the place is everywhere, and the people are you wonderful people right here."

"So," he continued enthusiastically, "what does that all mean? It seems like you have it all wrapped up." Marcus smiled and walked away from the rostrum into the group of delegates. He particularly moved to the side of a colourful group of Buddhist monks from Thailand. The only upbeat person in the room was the Dalai Lama, who seemed to be both respectful of the atrocities forced on the group and happy with the place both the event and he personally were in. He was always happy where he was in this life, with the safety of knowing it was one of many that he had partaken in and perhaps just the start of the future of more to come.

"How are you, gentlemen?" Marcus had reached out his hand to shake hands with a Thai monk and was greeted with hands in the traditional prayer structure. "OK." He quickly realised he didn't really know the culture of the monks and didn't really know where they were from, but he was quick on his feet and moved his hands in a prayer structure.

"So. From my first look at this, I was just spitballing a few ideas, thinking inside and outside the box, and trying to gauge the appetite of the room. I would say we are looking at a few key agenda items." He stopped next to the Baptist Ministry delegation and said, "How are you, brother? I am very pleased to see you here representing our fair state of Virginia."

The Baptist minister smiled emphatically.

He moved to the next slide, which had three dots on it and was titled 'Things in Common'.

The slide just had three dot points. Faith. God. Organisation.

"One. You are all in the same business. You have faith in God. You may call it a path to enlightenment, devotion, submission, or expression of the covenant, but they are all collectively your faith in whatever entity you choose. Allah, Yahweh, Buddha, etc. etc."

A few shocked sighs passed through the room as the object of the collective devotion of some four billion people was etc. etc. over.

"The truth is, you all have without a doubt the greatest organisations in the world. Whether they are democratically elected, decentralised, autocratic, or whatever, you people get things done on a global scale."

Marcus paused, hoping for applause. But instead got silent nodding.

"Education, aged care, youth support, you feed tens of millions daily, you clothe and shelter the needy. The list goes on, and I haven't even brushed on the ceremonial side, weddings, funerals, daily or weekly prayer."

Marcus paused again, seeing that the room wasn't going to applaud again, he applauded and encouraged the room to congratulate itself.

"Give yourself a round of applause. That's just fantastic, what an effort."

Marcus walked back past the Buddhist monks, who were applauding enthusiastically and smiling brightly and emphatically, and he encouraged them to continue as he made his way back to the rostrum.

"So," he continued, "this ought to be a snap as you all just have this all worked out." He said this as he mounted the stage and stood stoically behind the rostrum.

"But." He lowered his tone and stared into nowhere in particular to add some gravitas to the theatrics he unwound.

"If I may say one thing I have noticed, it is that even though you all have so much more in common than not, you do find it difficult to agree."

Marcus moved to the next slide, which had 'Problems' in big bold letters; the words had a picture underneath of a stick man looking pensive, and then the key points of dietary differences, the hierarchy of gods, saints, events, and key sites.

"So," Marcus continued, "I see we can either attempt to flesh these things out, say for the next *one thousand years*." He moved the microphone very close to his mouth to blur the words one thousand years.

"Then we probably will just not get anywhere."

Jessica was white as a sheet now. Where was this going?

"Or. We can cut the dogma and move on optimistically with what we need to do to combat the growing faith in the Greens and get the faithful back at your table."

"Hell yeah!" shouted the Baptist delegate from Virginia.

"That's what I'm talking about," Marcus responded gleefully. He was good at this and just needed someone in his audience to keep the momentum going. He moved swiftly from behind the rostrum to the front of the stage, waving his arms like he was bringing geese into the gated area around a farmhouse.

Most of the group looked shocked that someone would call on 'Hell' in such an enthusiastic and positive manner. Many of the translators, who up until this moment had been busily translating everything said, just kept silent.

"So." Marcus moved on, "What we need is to create a team that can take down the other team. Provide alternative leadership to the faithful to show them that those tricksters are not all they seem and that we are the one-stop shop. On a side note, I read today that in Sweden, do we have any Swedes here?" Marcus paused.

"No, OK. Anyway, Sweden has recently found that wind farms and solar just can't keep up with the country's power needs. The Greens had their chance, but the solution didn't cut it. One zip to us, I say."

Marcus raised his fist in the air defiantly.

Imam Hasan had also read that activists in Sweden had burned copies of the Quran.

One all maybe.

Anyway, to do this, we don't focus on differences. If you want to eat pork and you don't," Marcus pointed to a Presbyterian and a Scientologist, both of whom consumed pork.

"Then it's OK. Such things are cultural and regional and don't get written into the ideology at a high level. If you say your God is the one and only God and I say my God is the one and only God and all others are lesser in their divine status, well, maybe, just maybe, we are both right, and in one country, this God is just more active, and the reality is that other Gods just have their focus elsewhere."

Most of the interpreters were a bit lost; some had reverted to silence again. Some others chatted with other interpreters to clarify what some of Marcus' terms were. Others prattled on endlessly about things they thought the delegates would want to hear. Most of the interpreters spoke six or seven languages. Many of them were religious, affiliated with different traditions and spiritual beliefs; some were even ordained.

All were perplexed.

Feeling like he was finally getting things moving. Marcus continued, "The truth is, people are looking for what you can offer. All these great things you do, maybe they see them, maybe they don't. If you are providing blankets to the poor in the highlands in Scotland, what does anyone know about that when they are sitting on the beach in Cancun?"

The Mexican Catholic Cardinal had been starting to doze off. He wasn't tired, just bored. He had found a fantastic coffee shop across from the convention centre run by a Latino couple who were from Los Angeles. They had made him the most wonderful Mexican coffee, laden with heavy cream, whipped cream, brown sugar, and chocolate syrup. When he heard the name Cancun, he stood up and shouted. "Ariba Mexico!"

"That's what I am talking about." Marcus was happy that the crowd was getting involved and clapped his hands in encouragement. This was a very quiet bunch, and he was finally making some headway.

The Filipino Cardinal had been sitting next to his Mexican associate but hadn't had the benefit of the sugar-laden coffee the Mexican Cardinal had consumed. He was also drifting off as his interpreter was going on about everyone moving to another country if they didn't believe in the one god and Jesus Christ, our saviour. Moving to a country where your other God is watching you because Jesus just can't be everywhere. The Cardinal had a distinct advantage over many of the other delegates. He didn't listen to the interpreter because he needed it; far from it, he spoke perfect English. The Cardinal just liked to ensure that what was being interpreted and relayed to millions of other Filipinos was correct. After all, this was being broadcast live on Catholic radio to millions of the faithful in English and Tagalog.

He had worked with this Tagalog interpreter in particular before and had previously had to reprimand him for his blasphemous language. He decided that saying that our Lord Jesus Christ followed boundaries set and fought over by lesser men over history was one such time, and so he stood up to move to the upper level where the interpreters were seated to admonish him.

Just as he got up, someone from the back of the auditorium shouted out "What Rubbish" in a very loud voice.

"Well, I'm sorry you feel that way, sir." Marcus moved from the rostrum to greet the Cardinal, who turned, realising that it looked like he had stood up to say "What Rubbish" and was now leaving.

"That was not me sir," he said. "that comment came from the back somewhere." He realised it sounded like he was making excuses but persisted. "I am just going to the restroom."

He looked like he was lying, and it was called by Marcus, who pointed in the opposite direction where the sign clearly marked the WC. The Cardinal moved on in the direction Marcus pointed out to try to look less guilty, hoping he could double back to the upper levels once outside.

"Well," Marcus continued, "there are bound to be some detractors, but the fact is, if we want this to work, we must band together. Do what you do because you do a great job, but do it under a single banner and allow the world to see the awesome work you do in the name of your God."

"So." Marcus had been building to this, just trying to time it right. He thought he had it until the Filipino Cardinal stood up, but he had no time to reset.

He had been saving this line for the crescendo. "How can we unite the faithful if we have no united faith to preach?"

There were nods all around the room.

Many people who had earlier been confused and perhaps even a little put out by some of the things Marcus had said, found great value in this.

Marcus saw his chance and moved the slide to show the "proposed" name of the new converged religious body.

"This is '**THE FAITH**'!" he exclaimed using his best mystical voice, booming it out like he was presenting a band in some 80s nightclub.

"I did a quick check, and the dot-com website isn't being used and 'is' for sale."

Marcus felt he was on a winner and proceeded very quickly now.

"All organisations will sign on to a faith charter. I would suggest a total restructuring of all of your key organisations. Large religions with fifteen million followers or more are given voting rights. The key religions are given a veto. There is a unanimous cessation of the building of any new venues until a full audit and suitability survey are done on all existing sites. Existing sites will be evaluated for branding if chosen. We are looking for one hundred percent coverage and saturation in big power centres."

There were a lot of very blank faces, so Marcus continued.

"The faith charter will mandate "The Faith" and its members to maintain international harmony, uphold the sanctity of the faith, achieve "higher standards of living" for believers, address "economic, social, health, and related problems", and promote "universal respect for and observance of matters of faith and fundamental freedom of worship. As a charter and constituent treaty, its rules and obligations are binding on all members and supersede those of any other currently held or implied treaties."

"Honestly," Marcus held his hands up in a sign of peace, "I just banged this together on the way here. The finalised wording will obviously take some considerable time to work through."

Like a wave crashing on the stage, beginning as an echo, then cascading into a mammoth wall of noise, every delegate started orating simultaneously. Many had problems with restructuring, many with having no powers or losing the power they already had, and some were worried that a lifetime of servitude to their true, unique style of faith was now undulating into the distant horizon of generalisation.

Marcus waited patiently.

He was a seasoned keynote speaker and not new to controversy. He had them where he wanted them.

"I know this is a lot to take in; let's slide this one in too before we close for questions today. This is just the first small step on the long journey you will take to regain the faith of the people. Trust me, the most important part of the journey will be the colour. At the moment, you are all over the place, so we need to consolidate."

Now this was something Marcus felt good about, namely because Melissa in his office had been awake all night putting together some awesome graphics on the colours of all religions.

It turns out the religions of the world were indeed very colourful. Flags of the faiths ranged through oranges and yellows, blues and greens, purples, and reds. As a group, the flags of the religions perfectly represented the clashes of life between religious organisations and the historical path that led them all here.

As part of her work, Melissa had put together a montage of all the flags, and Marcus let it sit on the screen to let each delegate identify the flag of their faith.

Like a religiously universal 'Where's Wally?'

"So we are going up against a lobby that has labelled itself green. So keep that in mind. Anything green is **out**. Sorry Islam." Marcus turned to look to his left at no one in particular.

"Our research also shows that you should distance yourself from the LGBTQ+ rainbow flag, so any homogenisation of colours is also out. Any attempt to copy the mix of colours from the religious flags should be kept to an absolute minimum."

"Green is out!" Imam Hasan groaned loudly. "That is the colour of the prophet."

"Now hold on to that sir. I know everybody wants to bring forward what they have, but that one is a no-go. But work with me here. Green is a blended colour, so it's important that a primary colour be chosen. Red, blue, or yellow. You want to show you are the original and the best, united in one true faith, not to be broken down any further. Again, from our research, most of you already chose from these three colours, so now we are down to the choice of three, or are we?"

Marcus was again trying to build tension.

He moved to Melissa's next slide which was a pie chart of how many religions use each colour, next to one showing how many of the faithful belong to each colour.

He took a little bit too long looking at Melissa's great graphics and didn't notice the entire Islamist group led by the Iranian Mawlawi Abdolhamid Ismaeelzahi making for the exit. The Mawlawi had tried to sit through the meeting; he had never liked Imam Hasan, but he had promised him he would come. But this latest blasphemy was too much. He had looked around at the other Muslim delegates and made hand signals to get them to indicate their agreement that they should go. He had finally gotten the entire Muslim contingent to concur, and they walked out unified. Hasan's frustration had also reached a boiling point with the whole thing, and as much as he wanted to stay, he had to agree that this was preposterous.

Retrospectively, it was an amazing time for Islam. Unity amongst its own has always been difficult to achieve, but in the face of such adversity, the prophet's choice of favourite colour did indeed provide a miracle.

"Gentleman, please." Marcus had noticed them too late, and he only managed the words as the group of fifty had walked through the large swinging doors at the rear of the auditorium.

Marcus stood on the stage. Unsure of what he said to cause a walkout, he was determined to hold everybody else here.

"So the truth is that the colour of God needs to be red." He blurted out, waiting to gauge the room. He changed the slide to show Melissa's concluding graph showing that red was the most common colour across all religions and when matched with the percentages of the faithful that those religions represented, it was a clear standout.

At the bottom of the slide Melissa had created an awesome example flag having a red background with an intertwined Christian cross, Islamic crescent, and Hindu Bhagwa Dhwaj inscribed in black across the middle of the flag.

Methodists and Shaivist Hindus got up and made for the exit.

With Yitzakh unable to hold them back and led by the Sephardi Rabbi, the Jews also followed. Like Hasan, Yitzakh felt it was better to show unity with his brothers and followed with his head bowed.

Not being sure, but not seeing Saffron anywhere and thinking perhaps the conference was over, the majority of the Buddhists also got up and started to walk out before the Dalai Lama implored them to return to their seats.

Who refuses the Dalai Lama?

Jessica was distraught.

"Catholics are still here." She consoled herself.

"Let's let it play out. Red was their colour, so that should make this acceptable."

Marcus' face was ashen; he was crestfallen as thirty to forty percent of the audience had now walked out.

He really thought he had this.

"We thought we could add some base colours to play it off, mostly black and white, maybe some gold, but we don't want to appear too ostentatious."

His voice cracked as he pleaded out the rest of his endeavours.

His attempts at recovery floundered, and even though they were to be considered fringe, the Seventh-Day Adventists and Mormons got up to walk out, as did many of the other Protestants. Years of playing to tough crowds of disbelievers, cynics, and pessimists had simply not prepared Marcus for a mass walkout. He was expecting dissension, arguments, and even some heated debate, but they had all just left. He was almost complete but wasn't sure he could continue; his confidence had deflated to rock bottom.

He waited for a moment and happened to catch the eye of Jessica, who he noticed was also white as a sheet.

She had gotten up, but not to walk out. He watched her as she walked to the side of the auditorium and hand-signalled him to focus on the Catholics. She gave a thumbs-up and mouthed clear words. "Almost there."

Marcus took heart.

"So. There we are, 'the faith', wrapped in the colour red. Let's look at it as a great contrast in opposition to the colour green. If you happen to follow the beautiful game of soccer, it's Manchester United against Celtic."

That comment may have captured a great deal of interest in the room earlier. Even though Hasan and the Muslims and Yitzakh and the Jews were gone, this one line did resonate with Victor.

"So we are United, my son." Victor said. He knew his football. "In this world you envisage."

"Yes indeedy." Marcus grasped heartily at that thin thread, holding it in his grasp like the boy with his finger in the dyke, attempting to save the whole circus from unravelling.

"I like it," said Victor, who had the biggest smile on his face. "So what's next?" he asked.

"Well, there is just the question of finances, your holiness."

Marcus looked at the Cardinal sheepishly. Marcus wasn't exactly sure who this guy was, but he seemed to be in charge of the Catholic delegation, so did that make him the Pope?

The cardinal smiled, almost like the grin of a small child. Such a small slip-up in front of all the other cardinals is very nice.

"Not yet, my son. You can call me your eminence." He snickered, just loud enough for the two cardinals closest to him to hear. "What sort of finances are we talking about?"

"Well, your eminence, our estimates are that the collective faith organisations have well over a trillion dollars or euros in assets and draw a total income of around five hundred billion annually. No one keeps super tight records, and there are always a lot of write-downs, expenditures before tax, and some fairly shady accounting on the periphery, but if we use that as a guide, it would get you a seat at the G20 if you wanted one."

Marcus thought carefully. "If you don't already have one," he smiled his best 'you know more than me' smile.

"Centrally managed or not." Victor said with that smile you see in a nightmare where you know you should run but you are unceremoniously glued to the spot.

Marcus felt his skin crawl, like he shouldn't be the one making this deal.

"Those details are still up for negotiation, I believe." Marcus was a seasoned professional negotiator, but he felt unevenly matched and looked around for some backup, or, preferably, a tag team partner. The remaining delegates were all sitting quietly, listening.

"Red, eh." Victor was not really aiming it as a question, so Marcus backed away and made his way back to the rostrum.

"Centralised management of the collective good." Victor was mulling over what he had heard and building up to something.

"Manchester United of the Faith World."

Marcus smiled back clumsily.

"Veto Powers." Victor's voice seemed to be rising gleefully.

"Remind me who gets Veto powers." Victor openly grinned at Marcus, similar to the grin he would use as a boy when he would pass on the collection plate.

Marcus swallowed painfully.

"Chances are that would be the Christians, Muslims, Hindus, and maybe Buddhists, based on the numbers I have."

"Which Christians?" Victor replied quickly.

A deathly silence had fallen over the room.

"Well." Marcus looked up at Jessica." The Jews have an interesting model of a rotating shared presidency, or there can be a voting structure, usually majority rules."

Marcus was very relieved that the time to close out the conference had been reached, and to confirm this, the auditorium bell chimed a weary farewell.

Jessica sighed.

Victor had a smile from ear to ear. His place in history was sealed.

"A thousand years of protest undermined, not a bad morning's work. I love it. We'll be in touch." Victor spoke with a voice that sounded like the handshake had happened and the deal was done.

With that, the cardinal got to his feet, and like a gaggle of geese already shrouded in red, the Catholics walked from the room behind him.

Chapter Twelve

Epilog

Some random person walking by had noticed Boris's body slumped in the alley and called an ambulance.

He was admitted with cerebral haemorrhaging and was totally unresponsive. He had no ID on him, and no one came to claim him. He lay in a vegetative state until dental tests identified him. The hospital called his distraught parents, and lifeless, he was transferred to Barking Hospital to be close to them.

In a strange unexplained phenonenum no stars shone over the hospital that night.

Boris's sister Naina, his nephew Aeta, his parents William and Norma, and his mother's new poodle Zeke, plus the kindly priest from the All Saints Parish Church, gathered around as the machine keeping Boris' body alive was switched off.

Ari and his "A" team were identified as possible assailants, but they had left the country and were never formally questioned or charged.

www.ingramcontent.com/pod-product-compliance
Lightning Source LLC
Chambersburg PA
CBHW020132180626
46810CB00004B/1513